Opal Fields Book 4

I0593727

# Her

# Hidden

# Bones

# Chapter 1

Jenny's skin tingled in the crisp air. Fine white vapour hovered with each exhale. The glimmer of early morning sunlight crested over the mounds of red, white and ochre dirt, discarded from local opal mines. A drilling rig cast a looming shadow, silhouetted against the rising sun on the hill.

The sound of a motor firing up in the distance echoed over the small, isolated town. The smell of eucalyptus oil and diesel hung in the dry, dirt filled air. The morning was cool, but the clear sky and bright golden glow promised the chill wouldn't last long.

Some months ago, the plains of Coober Pedy flooded with one torrential downpour, leaving the area swamped in deep, red mud. It was a stark contrast from the day she'd arrived to a stifling hot desert that turned every metal surface into a cook top. It was refreshing to finally be hugging her quilt at night and squeezing in a morning run before work.

She glanced at Nick, jogging comfortably beside her. He flashed her a quick grin before puffing out his cheeks and drawing in air. He was a cold, unfriendly stone wall, devoid of emotion when they first met. Amazing how quickly things can change.

'Ready for breakfast?' She was surprised she didn't sound breathless.

Slowing their pace, they jogged into the *Opal Inn Motel* carpark where Nick was staying on the weekends since fire had destroyed his home. The blaze ruined the beautiful William Creek Homestead. She struggled with the guilt. If he hadn't been helping her keep two witnesses safe, the stone house would still be standing in all its glory.

1

'You bet.' He leant forward with his hands on his knees to take a moment to adjust his breathing, then followed her to the reception area.

'Hey Marj.' She stuck her head into the office to see the red-headed busty motel owner sporting an even brighter shade of bottle red than usual. It was only outdazzled by her broad, genuine grin.

'Morning luv. You two are looking good.' She nodded at Nick. The motel owner was a born matchmaker. First, she tried to match Jenny up with the local doctor, Nev – who was now one of her two flat mates. Then Nick had fallen into her sights.

'Thanks Marj. I'll call in for a catch up before I head over to the station. I need to grab food first.' She rubbed her stomach.

'Of course.' Marj waved from her usual perch behind the reception counter. Even at seven a.m., the television played a US soap quietly in the background while Marj busied herself with paperwork. 'You get going, before you fade away.'

They strolled down the veranda as the sun came into view, casting sudden warmth over the artificial grassed courtyard. Jenny watched the stars blink out one by one as predawn gave way to daylight. Nick held the door open.

'How's the rebuild going?' She passed through.

'Good. The old stone survived the fire and we've sourced some reclaimed wood from Murphy's old shearing shed for the flooring beams and trusses.'

'You know how sorry I am. Right?'

'It wasn't your fault. I'm just glad we all made it out alive.'

'How's Sam coping?' Nick's brother was over ten years younger. They lost their parents around the same time her cousin and aunt went missing. The boys were on their own, with no other family close by.

Her missing family members were the reason she accepted the job in the outback opal mining town. The death of Nick's father and missing mother were right at the centre of her unofficial investigation into why Melanie and Aunt Carolyn never came home.

'Sam's decided it is the universe telling him to travel in his gap year.' Nick smiled again. Jenny's heart melted so see him happy. 'At least, that's his opinion while I'm living in the shearing quarters during the week. I'm sure once the house is rebuilt, he'll be home again.'

Jenny chuckled as they wandered to a small table in a quiet corner of the expansive dining area. Gouges worn in the commercial carpet frayed under the chair legs. They matched the nineteen seventies concertina doors and fake walnut wood panelling perfectly.

The motel could do with a revamp, but Coober Pedy consisted of opal claim owners, big mining fly in workers and a handful of businesses to support them and, of course, the seasonal tourist trade. Timber veneer floors, white subway tiles and black metal shelving brimming with fake green plants was not what the locals wanted from their regular bar.

'I've got an update on your dad's case. Before or after breakfast?'

'During.' Nick pulled out a chair for Jenny. She sat, her stomach rolled with confused emotions. Reopening the assumed suicide case, now murder case could be the key to discovering where Melanie and Aunt Carolyn were, but for Nick, it could also point the finger at his mother, who went missing the same day his dad died from a gunshot wound to the head.

'Coffee?' His voice snapped her mind back to the present.

'Thanks.' Nick approached the long breakfast buffet and poured two mugs of filtered coffee. It wasn't her favourite kick-starter, but it would hold her over until she could grab her regular caramel latte from Niko's café.

Nick placed the mugs on the table before sliding into his seat. 'What have you found?'

'We've got the report from the coroner's office and the forensic lab in Adelaide. They've collated all the findings.' She sipped her coffee.

'And?' Nick was yet to touch his.

Nearly two months prior, the forensic team agreed to exhume Nick's dad's body because a post-mortem was never conducted. The death was originally signed off as suicide, but once her friend, crime scene investigator Penny McGregor saw the photos taken after his death, she red-flagged the case.

'And they've officially reopened the case.' She watched his face contort with the bittersweet news. Finding out what happened to his dad was important. But she could see the idea his missing mother might be responsible was tearing him apart on the inside.

He let out a slow breath. 'Where do we start?'

'I'll go over it with Sarge today, but I don't think we'll get into it until next week. We run a skeleton staff on the weekend and deal with urgent cases only. I know you've waited a long time for this, but cold cases get squeezed in between current workloads.'

'I understand. Do you need anything from me?'

'Did you find anything else in the cellar after the fire?'

She searched the cellar with Nick on a few occasions for any link to confirm that her cousin Melanie and Aunt Carolyn stayed there as planned. The only evidence placing

Melanie on the property was a jackaroo stating he saw her with Nick's dad once, and her handwriting in an accounts ledger.

'Nothing new.' Nick lifted his coffee to his lips, stopped and frowned.

'I heard it.' She swung her head at the sound of screeching brakes, her heart skipping a beat. They leapt to their feet, running for the door as the building shuddered, and the sound of breaking glass and screams erupted.

'Out front!' Nick sprinted for the parking area in front of reception.

'Marj!' Debris scattered out over the artificial turf and native shrubs. Jenny coughed as dust settled on the scene.

'Call an ambulance!' Nick called to anyone within earshot.

Stan, the bartender and backbone of Marj's restaurant called from the doorway. 'Doing it.' Jenny noticed him punching buttons on his mobile phone.

'Marj! Can you hear me?' Jenny shimmied past the sedan tightly wedged inside the reception area. Broken cement bricks crumpled the roof of the vehicle. Timber, nails, concrete and plasterboard crunched under her feet as she inched her way toward the reception desk.

'Marj!' She called again, her heart pounded as she scanned the scene, Nick two steps ahead.

'What the hell!' Jenny's partner, Constable Philips skidded to a halt outside the building, his eyes scanning the mess. 'I heard it from the station. Came as quick as I could. What do you need?'

'Check the driver.' Jenny pointed at a thick mop of grey hair slumped over the steering wheel. Nick clambered over the bonnet ahead of her. 'We're looking for Marj. She was in here when I arrived.'

'She's always in here. Is the ambulance on the way?' Philips studied the back of the vehicle. The wall was crumbling on the driver's side, making it impossible for him to access the victim through the door.

'Yes. Stan's on the phone now.' Jenny followed Nick over the car bonnet as steam erupted from the radiator, lowering visibility and diverting her to a different route.

Jenny spotted Philips studying the broken rear window. She noticed the tiny pieces of laminated glass cubes scattered everywhere on her way past. She glanced back to see Philips hoist himself over the boot and gingerly wiggle through the rear window to assess the driver.

Shattered glass crunched under her feet as sweat dripped down her back, but all Jenny could think about was Marj. 'Hang on Marj, we're coming.'

A moan sounded ahead. 'Marj. It's Nick. I've got you.' Jenny joined him two seconds later.

'What hurts?' Jenny asked as she cleared debris from the older woman's face and Nick lifted the counter away. 'Can you breathe?'

'Everything hurts, but I'm okay.'

Marj lay jammed up against the wall, the stool she usually sat on was crumpled and embedded into the plasterboard behind the counter. Books were scattered, the TV, mounted to the wall was miraculously still on and going with a rerun of *Days of our Lives*.

Jenny's heart pounded in her chest as she lifted debris... helped Nick lever the counter away to make space so they could reach Marj.

'Ambulance is on the way.' Stan called from the collapsed side doorway, phone still to his ear in touch with the operator. Plasterboard and broken cement blocks left a greyish mist over every surface. 'And the SES.'

'Thanks Stan.' Jenny returned her gaze to her patient. 'The emergency boys will have you out in no time.' Jenny glanced over to check on Philips. 'How's the driver?'

'Ah.' Jenny frowned at the tone of Philips' voice. 'Driver's unconscious, but there's a pulse.'

Jenny questioned Marj with her eyes. The older woman gave her a weak smile. 'I'm good luv. You do your job.'

'I've got her,' Nick's eyes promised. The motel owner wasn't only a local resident needing her care. She was her mother away from home. When Jenny relocated to the desolate opal mining town, she stayed at the motel for the first month. Marj became her rock of stability from the moment she arrived. If anything happened to her. She shook her head, shoving negative thoughts aside. She had a job to do.

'What's up Philips?' Jenny carefully slid over the bonnet of the wrecked car to peer through the shattered windscreen. Her eyes widened as Philips pointed to matted grey hair protruding from a bundle of faded fabric.

'Where the hell did that come from?' Philips shrugged at Jenny's rhetorical question.

Alongside the driver's side door, amongst the broken cement bricks, glass and wooden framework, hidden beneath rough fabric was a pile of discoloured bones, shrivelled skin, tattered clothing and the unmistakable skull of a dead body.

'I don't think it was in the car?' Philips stated the obvious.

Sirens wailed in the distance as two khaki police uniforms peered into the fray.

'No shit Sherlock.' The gruff voice of their commanding officer spoke into the mayhem.

# Chapter 2

'I'm fine Jenny.' Marj gripped her hand as Tim, her other flat mate and local paramedic wheeled the gurney toward the waiting ambulance. 'How's the driver?'

Just like Marj to be more concerned about someone else.

'She's regained consciousness.'

'Oh, that's good.' A mischievous grin crossed her face as Tim prepared to push the gurney into the ambulance. 'Did I hear someone say they found a body?'

Most people who discovered a body buried in their walls for years would be distressed. Marj wasn't like most people because she was a self-confessed mystery junkie. If she wasn't watching some old rerun of *Murder She Wrote*, she was nose deep in a cosy mystery novel. But Jenny knew there would be nothing cosy about a body hidden away in the motel wall.

'You did. But don't you worry about it now.' Jenny tapped her hand as Tim pushed the gurney inside. 'There'll be plenty of time for your hypothesis when you get out of hospital.'

Tim gave her a nod, then closed the doors.

'She's stable. I think she might have fractured her arm, but thankfully her hips look good.'

'Thanks Tim. See you tonight.'

'You bet.' He peered over her shoulder at the wreckage. 'Do you think the bar will still be open later?'

She laughed. 'I think Stan will be putting on drinks for the entire CFS and SES team, so yes. I'll likely see you there.'

Jenny turned to see two Country Fire Service team members taping off the carpark and damaged building.

'Thanks guys. Can we get a tarp over the roof area?'

'Nah.' A CFS volunteer in yellow overalls held together by bulging buttons straining to contain his round belly, didn't seem willing to elaborate. His friend shook his head.

'The structure is unstable. We'll get one up if it looks like rain but it's clear as a bell out here.'

'Thanks Mick. Just trying to minimise any foreign evidence getting into the scene.'

'I hear you, but this is a pitched roof, not trussed. If we start climbing around up there, it could all come crashing down.'

'Good point.' Jenny wasn't about to argue with the guy. He was wearing the CFS volunteer uniform today, but Mick worked as a safety officer for the council and risk management was what he got paid for.

'Hey Mick. Who did the work on this building anyway?'

Mick shrugged. 'Probably Con. He's built just about every building in town, but…' He rubbed his chin, his eyebrows knitted together as he thought. 'Come to think of it, this isn't the first car to drive into Marj's front office. I reckon it was about five years back. Were you here then Frank?'

An SES worker was busy nearby. He glanced over. 'What's that?'

'Didn't we pull another car out of here a few years back?'

'Yep. Sure did. Should be on the police records Jenny. The boys at the station will remember.'

'Thanks guys. I'll get the dates. Did Con fix that hole up too?'

'Probably.' Both men answered in unison.

'Thanks.' She waved as she strode toward Nick, who was busy assisting the SES to cut open the sedan and retrieve the patient still trapped inside. The Jaws-of-Life squeezed. Metal crushed, squeaked and broke with each compression.

Jenny sighed as three SES operators gathered around the patient, operating the rescue equipment and monitoring her vital signs as they worked. Her crime scene was right under their feet, but there was nothing she could do about it. The patient needed to be removed from the vehicle. They couldn't tow it out while she was still inside, in case more debris came down.

Each step on the driver's side was right over the top of the victim. They placed planks of wood over the remains before they started the rescue operation, but the Adelaide forensic team were going to have their work cut out for them on this one.

Thinking of Penny coming to town for the investigation made her relax. It was always great to catch up with the scientist. It was a shame it was usually over a dead body.

'When's Penny due in?'

Sergeant Mackenzie glanced at his watch. 'She'll be a few hours. I'll pick her up from the airport and bring her straight out to the scene.'

Jenny nodded. 'I'll give her a hand here then.'

'O'Connell will look after the station for now. I'll take over after I've picked up McGregor. Philips, you get the rescue team whatever they need and take charge of the crime scene log.'

Philips nodded, and shuffled past Jenny. 'Murder Magnet.' He whispered loud enough for everyone within ear shot to hear.

Senior Constable O'Connell dropped his head, to peer over his reading glasses at her. 'Four murders in six months must be a record.' He then focussed back on signing out on the crime scene log and handed it to Philips.

'You two are full of it.' Since moving to the remote town, she'd racked up four cases involving suspicious deaths. Tiffany Cox, Beth Thompson, Melinda Smart and now whoever this poor victim was. Apparently murder never happened before she came to town.

The fact Tiffany Cox died six months before she arrived, and whoever was in the wall of Marj's office was hidden away when the last repairs were done, should count for something. *Shouldn't it?*

'Five.' Sarge corrected.

'Five what?' She frowned.

'Murders. We've just officially reopened Ron Johnston's case remember.'

# Chapter 3

Nick sighed as Jenny handed him a bottle of water. His running gear was covered in dust, his hair spotted with pieces of plasterboard. 'I'm guessing our weekend date is cancelled.'

'I'm sorry.' She sipped her water and slumped down alongside him on the garden wall.

'It's okay. It's your job. I get it.' He surveyed the scene. Only one SES unit remained, with a skeleton crew on hand to help ensure nothing caved in while they assessed the scene and recovered the body.

'I'll try and drive out tomorrow.' She reached for his hand. His fingers entwined between hers.

'It's alright.' She could see he wanted to smile but couldn't. It seemed her work or his responsibilities at the station got in the way at every turn. 'I'll head out to Mrs B.'s. I need to help with rebuilding the units out there in any case.'

'I'll see if I can meet you out there, even if it's only for a few hours on Sunday.'

'It's a long way to go for a few hours.'

'I think you're worth it.' She squeezed his hand, leant forward and waited for his eyes to meet hers. 'As much as I want to kiss you right now.'

'I know.' He scanned the area over her shoulder. 'You're working.'

'Bugger it.' She released his hand, grabbed his face firmly with her hands, leant in and kissed him. He didn't resist.

'Williams!' The sound made her jump, but it wasn't who she expected to hear grumbling at her.

'Take your hands off him. You don't know where he's been.' Nick chuckled softly. Jenny touched her nose to his, kissed him again, then laughed aloud as Penny strode up in her long, ungainly farmgirl style. 'You've got work to do.'

'I'm not even in uniform yet.' She pointed to her tank top and leggings, still sweaty, but now covered in dirt and debris from the accident scene.

'You don't need a uniform to assist me.' Penny handed her a pair of gloves. 'I'm guessing the scene is a mess.'

'You're guessing right. Two accident victims needed to be evacuated before we could lock it down. I'm sorry, but the SES traipsed all over the place. We covered the victim as best we could.'

Penny's face turned serious. 'Is Marj okay?'

'Shocked, battered, bruised. Maybe a broken arm Tim reckons, but she was really lucky.'

'And the driver?'

'Miraculously unscathed. Poor old dear hit the accelerator instead of the brake by the sounds of it. She did lose consciousness though, so the boys are running scans. We'll interview her to confirm after they finish.'

'Well, dead bodies get right of way. Let's go.'

Jenny let her hand slip away from Nick's. 'See you tomorrow.'

'Promise?'

'You know I'll do everything I can.' She turned and followed Penny, trying not to look back at Nick's eyes. She knew without checking, the mask would be back up, covering his emotions. It was his way of coping, ever since his dad died. Or maybe he was always serious?

'Here, put these on.' Penny handed her a pair of shoe covers and disposable overalls. 'Probably a waste of time, but.'

Penny stopped outside the scene, drew her camera from a bag, pulled gloves on and began taking photos around the perimeter of the building.

Working her way in, she tried to carefully pick her way over the debris without dislodging anything. 'I'm going to need backup on this one.'

'I can help collate evidence.' Jenny offered as she held up a piece of broken plasterboard and lifted the wooden planks away for Penny to photograph the victim.

'Not on this one. I'll get a few techs here to help dismantle the building piece by piece. We need to make sure we collate everything so we can work out where in the wall she was stashed and collect all the trace evidence. Even a hair, a piece of jewellery, or a pen encased in the wall with the victim could be vital. We need it all.'

Jenny sighed. It was a huge job. She flinched. 'Did you say *she*?'

'I did. Obviously, we'll need to get her out and let Doc confirm, but my money is on our victim being female.'

'So someone killed a woman. Hid her in the wall of Marj's office approximately five years ago.'

'Five years?'

'Yeah. A few of the SES and CFS guys said this very wall was rebuilt after a similar accident about five years ago.

'In that case. Get out of here and go visit the builder. This woman was wrapped in plastic to keep the smell down and,' she pointed to a piece of timber near the woman's hand, 'nailed to the framework to keep her in place.'

'Is that a pneumatic gun nail?'

'That's my guess.'

Jenny scrunched her nose up. 'That's awful. I hope she was dead when it happened.'

'Me too.'

14

# Chapter 4

Jenny left Penny to finish the evidence gathering, crossed the road toward the police station and tried to ignore half a cup of coffee gurgling in her stomach. Glancing at her watch, she realised lunch was probably going to have to wait. She didn't function well on an empty stomach but she was late for a briefing.

The smell of steak pies and tomato sauce overloaded her senses as she opened the police station front door.

'Just in time. Should have known you'd sniff out the food.' Philips lifted a pie bag in salute, his face scattered with filo pastry crumbs grinned up at her.

'Oh my god. Did Niko bring those in?' She rushed to the counter, lifted the moveable top and let it slam behind her. Ignoring the pile of brown paper bags stained in sauce, she made a beeline for the cardboard tray of *real* coffee.

Her usual caramel latte was lovingly labelled with a *J* inside a heart. 'I'm starving, but I desperately need this.' She longingly sipped her coffee, eyes closed, her nose twitching with the aroma.

'Where are we with an ID? Anything on the victim?' Sarge sat on the corner of the communal desk. O'Connell occupied the chair.

She opened her eyes, her brain kicked into gear. 'Penny hasn't found anything on scene?' Jenny glanced from face to face, finally resting on Senior Constable O'Connell. 'But she suggested we start questioning the builders. The victim was nailed to the stud wall frames, then plasterboard was put up to encase her.'

'Her.' Sarge stopped chewing for a split second.

'Penny thinks we have a female victim, but she'll need the Doc to confirm.'

'Cause of death?'

'Not yet. But we barely uncovered the body Sir. Penny has requested a forensic anthropologist and another crime scene tech to help bag and tag all the debris. Evidence could be anywhere.'

'It's going to take a month of Sundays to sift through that lot.' O'Connell perused the coffee tray, finding a cup labelled for him.

Jenny's stomach grumbled loudly. 'Eat something Williams, before you fade away,' Sarge insisted as he peeked inside a brown bag, his brow creasing as he decided on which variety of pie he would consume next.

'Has anyone heard about Marj?' She found a chicken pie, thankfully without sauce. In her opinion, no one should ever eat chicken pie with tomato sauce.

'Nev called.' The local doctor grew up in the area and knew Marj well. Jenny was relieved he was on duty, looking after the vivacious motel owner. 'Said they set her arm. She was bumped around, but all in one piece.'

'I took a photo of the victim. Should I ask her if she recognises her? The woman was hidden in her office wall afterall?' Jenny filled her mouth with a large bite of her pie, chewed, sighed, then spoke through the mouthful. 'These are *so* good.'

'I know. Niko is a whizz in the kitchen.' Philips finished his pie, screwed up the paper, then looked around for something to wipe his hands on. Finding nothing, he used his pants. Jenny frowned. He blushed self-consciously.

'Finish your food, then head over to the hospital. Show Marj the photo, see what she says and if she's ready to be discharged, drop her around to my place for the night. Her unit will be a mess from the accident and it's going to take a while before we can find her a room key to a spare unit at the motel amongst all the debris.'

'I've got Nick's unit key Sarge. He's heading back home since I'm going to be busy.'

'Okay. That'll do.' Her commanding officer didn't seem the least bit guilty she was missing another weekend with Nick. 'Confirm who the builder was, the one who worked on the repairs to the office while you're at it.'

'It was Con. I'm sure of it.' Philips offered.

'I know you are all locals, but how about a full name, business details for the newbie here?' Jenny pointed to her chest.

'Con Papadakis. His business name is *Papa Construction*. But they won't be open today.'

'We'll follow up with them Monday.' Sarge stood, brushed his chest clean of pastry crumbs and strolled around his desk toward the front door. 'It's going to take McGregor and her team all weekend to get through that debris. I'll chat to Frank with the SES and ask them to have a small team work with her to clear away anything she needs and secure the building as she goes.'

'You finishing up then Sir?' O'Connell threw his empty coffee cup in the bin alongside the desk.

'Our victim has been dead at least five years. Another few days won't make or break the case. I'm heading out to Murphy's property. With the Johnston case reopened, I've got a few follow up questions I'd like to ask Kent about Ron and Patricia Johnston.'

Jenny wanted to be a fly on the wall for *that* conversation, but she knew Sergeant Mackenzie and Kent Murphy's relationship went back at least two decades and he was fiercely protective of his friends when it came to police business.

When she first met Kent, she immediately struggled to trust him, but she was investigating a missing woman linked to his son at the time. When Nick was shot, bleeding out on Kent's kitchen floor, he proved to be strong and supportive. He also mentioned Nick was tough, like his mum. She missed the reference at the time, but since the ordeal, the comment had rattled around in her mind.

Her gut instincts told her Kent Murphy knew more about Patricia Johnston's disappearance. Nick suspected his mum and Kent might have been romantically involved, but Jenny saw something else in Kent's eyes that day. It wasn't lust, it was respect. Maybe Kent held the key to finding out what happened to her aunt and cousin too, but if he did, why was he keeping it to himself?

'I'm out of here then.' Jenny tossed her empty coffee cup in the bin, snatched another pie and headed for the door.

# Chapter 5

Jenny parked her vintage Dodge utility in the hospital carpark. Stepping out, she pressed the lock button and slammed the heavy door shut. Spotting Nev under the emergency awning, assisting outside an ambulance, she waved. He smiled and returned the gesture.

As much as she wanted to stop and quiz him about Marj's condition, she could see he was occupied with a patient.

Manoeuvring her way through the Ambulance Entrance, she avoided the waiting room and triage registry nurse. No one would challenge her, even if she wasn't in uniform. All the staff at the hospital knew who she was now. After nearly six months in town, she'd either been on an accident site, met the staff at the motel restaurant or been introduced by Nev or Tim to every nurse, doctor and paramedic in the small, remote community.

Her running shoes squeaked on the white and grey lino floor as she entered the triage ward. The smell of bleach made her nose itchy. She rubbed it with the back of her hand while she checked the text message from Marj. Scanning the cubicles, her eyes rested on the last one on the left.

'Marj. You still in there?' The blue, disposable curtain was drawn.

'Yep. All set to go luv.' Jenny pulled the curtain back to find her friend sitting up on the crisp white sheets.

'I managed to pick up a few things for you to wear. Your place is locked up until they secure the site, sorry.' She handed a small gym bag over.

'I'm good to go.' Jenny scanned the woman in her striped hospital robe and chuckled.

'You do know your arse is going to hang out the back all the way to my car?' Jenny opened the bag zip and drew out a pair of pants. 'Get changed into the bottoms, slip on the button up shirt, then give me a call and I'll button it up for you.' Jenny waggled her finger at the older woman. 'No arguments. I'm not taking you out of here like that.'

Marj's cheeky expression spread to her eyes. 'I don't know. There's a spunky looking gentleman called Mr Jones in the end bed on the right. I was planning on putting on a show.' Her eyebrows wriggled.

Jenny recalled Marj's birthday celebration. The woman was in her sixties, but her fuller figure didn't stop her looking amazing in a black leotard with a sequined waist coat. Her skin tingled as Marj's rendition of *Big Spender*, Liza Minelli style came to mind. It was quite a night and Marj was not a shy woman.

'I'd have to arrest you for indecent exposure if you did.' Jenny focussed on keeping a dead pan face. Marj's eyes grew wide.

'You wouldn't!'

Jenny shook her head, her expression firm. 'You'd give me no choice.'

Marj grabbed the bag and huffed. 'In that case.' She shooed Jenny from the cubicle.

Five minutes later, without any help, Marj strolled out from behind the curtain, her arm in a sling.

'You'll flash for Mr Jones in bed six, but won't let me help you button up your shirt?'

'A woman has pride you know.' Marj passed Jenny's gym bag back to her and pranced past Mr Jones with an exaggerated hip sway.

Jenny followed, shaking her head and not at all surprised to see Mr Jones paying close attention. *Mrs* Jones didn't look impressed.

Jenny opened the door and held it as Marj exited the hospital. The woman certainly knew how to draw attention to herself.

'I've got a photo to show you when I get you home.'

'You said I can't go home.' Jenny opened the passenger side of her Dodge and waited for Marj to wriggle into her seat.

'Here, nurse this.' Jenny handed her the bag. 'Nick has gone back to the William Creek Pub since I got a little tied up.'

'Oh, sorry luv.'

'Not your fault.' Jenny pulled the door, which creaked in protest as she slammed it shut. The vintage Dodge was old in a good way, but it was rough as guts and needed some serious body work – something she didn't have time for right now.

Jenny slipped into the driver's seat, flattened the accelerator to the floor twice, then held it down and turned the motor over. Thankfully it kicked to life on the first attempt because the battery was close to flat.

'Nick left me with the key to his room. We couldn't find any other keys to the spare rooms amongst the mess, so Stan organised for clean bed linen and it's ready for you.'

'What photo have you got? Is it the dead woman?'

Jenny opened her mouth, then closed it. 'How do you know it was a woman?' She studied Marj's face a moment, before putting on her indicator and pulling out onto the main road back into town.

'I hear things.'

'For goodness' sake Marj. You've been in hospital with a broken arm and still you've managed to pick up gossip the team only discussed a few hours ago. How on earth do you manage it?'

Marj grinned and tapped her nose. 'My secret source.'

'Have you bugged our office or something?'

'Or something.'

Jenny pulled into the service carpark at the motel, turned off the motor and jumped out to help Marj out of the car. She should have known it was a useless gesture. The woman was out and on her feet before Jenny got to the passenger's side door.

'Forget the room. I need a brandy.' She wandered through the rear door into the commercial kitchen. The back side of the restaurant was new to Jenny. Her eyes scanned the surfaces loaded with fresh food. A shorter man, with olive skin and thick black hair spoke to a heavy-set woman in Spanish or some sort of South American language Jenny didn't understand.

'Mateo. I'll have a chicken parmy and grab a chicken pasta pesto for Jenny. Thanks.'

'Marj. You good?' She nodded. 'Groso.'

'Gracias Mateo.'

They continued along the commercial vinyl floor, past the cool room and out into the dining area. Marj didn't miss a beat as Jenny jogged to keep up.

'Brandy thanks Stan.' Marj dragged out a stool, sat, held out her good hand, elbow resting on the bar and waited without a word until the tumbler of brandy was in her hand. 'This'll calm the nerves.' She sculled it in one mouthful, slammed the glass down. 'Top it up Stan.' Turning to Jenny she tapped the bench. 'Okay. Let's have it.'

'You sure?' Jenny pulled out a stool and joined Marj.

'Luv. There's no time like the present. I've been sharing my office with a dead body since the office was repaired, so I may as well meet my roommate.' She tapped the bar again as her second brandy arrived.

Jenny glanced at Stan, who wore a grin from ear to ear. Shaking her head, she drew her mobile phone from her pocket, pressed her screenlock code, opened her photo gallery and pulled up the last photo in her gallery.

A skeletal face, with hollow eye sockets stared back at her. Placing it on the bar, facing Marj she prepared herself to catch the woman in case she fainted. She should have known better. The former opal miner didn't flinch. Not even so much as a screwing up of her nose.

Instead, she rubbed her chin, tapped her finger on her lip and sighed. 'I can't be sure, but if I was a betting woman.' Stan scoffed. 'Okay, I have a flutter on the ponies occasionally.' She shook her finger at her bartender.

Tension left Jenny's shoulders with Marj's expression. 'You think you know her?'

'I'll let your scientists confirm. I might be able to point you in the right direction though. It's hard to tell for sure.' Marj studied the photo, zoomed in on the fabric of the woman's top, then puffed out her cheeks, and studied some more. Jenny's patience was almost spent. She opened her mouth to push, as Marj spat out the words she never expected to hear.

'It's my sister-in-law, Franny.'

# Chapter 6

'You sure?' Stan snatched up Jenny's phone, squinted and zoomed in the picture with his fingers. 'Shit. It does look like her fancy silk flower top. Can't be many of them in town.'

'I wondered where she went, but to be honest, I was just happy she racked off.' Marj swigged her brandy.

'What do you mean?' Jenny held her hand out for her phone. Stan's hand hovered, his mouth open. He visibly shook himself to clear his head.

'Hey Marj. Maybe you shouldn't say anything.' Stan's posture changed. The bartender was usually the epitome of casual, but his body was rigid, his eyes thoughtful.

'Oh Stan. I've got nothing to hide. I had a full on barny with *that* woman over Jason's estate. It's common knowledge. No point hiding it. If someone did her in, it will all come out. Jenny here,' she reached over, resting her hand proudly on Jenny's shoulder, 'is a top-notch investigator.' The brandy must have been kicking in. Marj was getting sentimental.

'Stan's right though Marj.' She suddenly felt protective. 'You should probably consult a lawyer first.'

'Are you supposed to be telling me that?' Marj winked as Stan topped up her brandy, which she drank without even looking at the glass.

'Well I'm not formally interviewing you. Yet. As soon as I tell the boss who this is, we'll have to make this official and if you were seen arguing with the victim, well...' Marj waved her hand.

'I told you. I never touched Franny. She was a piece of work though. I think you'll find enemies on every corner of *this* town.'

'Let's leave the gossip out of it for now Marj.' Jenny wanted to change the subject and give Marj time to consider her options. If the victim was her sister-in-law and they argued over money, Marj would ultimately be a prime suspect and there was nothing about interviewing her friend that felt good.

'How about you confirm who did the office repairs? Whoever sealed up the walls must have known the body was there.'

'Con and *Papa Construction* did the work, but he wouldn't have killed Franny.'

'I'll need to find out who did the work anyway.'

'There better be some seriously good entertainment tonight Marj.' Penny's voice rose above the quiet hum as she strode toward the front bar.

'How about another round of Karaoke?' Marj grinned, Penny scoffed and Jenny searched for a rock to hide under.

The photos of her, Penny and local doctor Nev were still popping up around the station from time to time. Living down her first night in town was never going to happen. There were too many beers, too much tension and way too many ABBA songs sung in the *Opal Inn Motel* that night.

'Count me out. I'm heading to Nick's place.' Jenny slipped off the bar stool.

Penny pouted. 'After dinner. Right?'

Penny was a party girl and Jenny tossed up if it was wise to hang around until after dinner, but she loved spending time with the forensic scientist and Nick would understand. He wasn't expecting her until Sunday anyway.

'A couple of beers. No Karaoke and an early night.' Jenny held her finger up. 'Deal?'

'Deal.' Penny turned to Stan. 'Can I grab a burger and a ginger beer? Thanks Stan. Non-alcoholic. I've still got at least five more hours of work to get through this afternoon.'

'How's it going out there?' Jenny steered her friend away from the bar. 'Marj might know the victim. Has she been removed yet?' Jenny peered over Penny's shoulder. Marj was showing little interest in the conversation, but there was no doubt in Jenny's mind she was listening. The woman was a walking, talking gossip machine.

'Nearly there. The team have cleared most of the debris around the body. I want to get her out before they remove the car. Then we'll have more sifting to do.'

'I've got to let O'Connell know about Marj's possible connection with the victim. Get some dental records organised for the coroner.'

'A possible ID will make life so much easier.'

'Drinks up Penny.' Stan lifted a schooner at the bar.

'I'll grab a quick lunch, get on with extricating the body and then touch base for drinks later tonight. Thanks for hanging around. It's not the same here without you.'

'I'll only be at Nick's for a few hours Sunday. I'll be back on deck Monday for work. I'm sure Tim can keep you busy.' Jenny grinned.

'He is a fun side-track when I'm in town.'

Jenny's roommate Tim and Penny shared history going back to their university days. Whenever she was in town, Penny always caught up with Tim, but the forensic scientist was career focussed and Tim was a long way from her Adelaide base.

Jenny often wondered if they'd ever make the relationship permanent. 'That's all he is then?'

Penny shrugged. 'He's here. I'm there. It is what it is.'

'Burger's up.' Penny scurried to the counter and reached for the white paper bag containing her lunch.

'Thanks Stan,' she called over her shoulder, then turned back to Jenny. 'See you after six.'

'You bet.' Jenny returned to the bar. 'Are you going to be okay?'

'I'm fine luv. Stan here will look after me. My pain meds are kicking in. I'll take a rest soon.'

'You do that.' Jenny patted her gently on the shoulder. 'I'll organise a formal interview Monday, so call a lawyer. Please!'

'I've already done it.' Stan interrupted.

'Thanks mate.'

'Oh stop fussing. Both of you.'

'See you later. Sorry, but I have to go.' Jenny waited, not wanting to leave her friend, but knowing the best way to protect Marj was to find out who really killed her sister-in-law, if that's who it turned out to be.

# Chapter 7

O'Connell's brow creased as he frowned down his nose, over his reading glasses at Jenny. 'Franny! She's sure?'

'Stan and she recognised the fabric in the victim's blouse. No guarantees, but it gives the coroner a place to start.'

'All right. Check to see if anyone reported her missing. Find a next of kin. Jason's gone, his mum or dad could be alive, but they'd be in their eighties or nineties by now. I'll organise a warrant for her medical records. Maybe we'll get a hit on dental records.'

'On it Sir.' Jenny rushed to the front counter computer and began typing Franny's details into the Australian Federal Police missing person's database.

The details churned through the system slowly. There were thousands of missing person reports filed annually in Australia. Most were found quickly, but Jenny knew there were over two and a half thousand unsolved cases currently on file.

Nothing came up. It made sense. If Franny was reported missing, Marj would have known about it and so would local police, although if Len Holmes handled a report, it was likely to have been mismanaged like everything else the former Senior Constable touched.

'Nothing coming up Sir.'

'Get a notice out to all dental practices locally, plus any near where Kovac lived in Adelaide. With any luck, Franny was seeing someone in town when she lived here.'

'Marj said she was here for Jason's Will reading. Did she live here before?'

'She travelled a lot, but I think she lived here at one point.'

'Hopefully luck is on our side then.' Jenny searched the vehicle registration and licensing office for the victim's last known address. While the search churned away, she opened a browser to find the local dentist.

Voices echoed through the police station entrance. She peered over the counter to see Philips and Penny enter, still in disposable overalls.

'What you got McGregor?' O'Connell adjusted his reading glasses down his nose so he could see distance more clearly.

'Not sure yet, but I think we found the murder weapon.' Penny held up a paper bag labelled and taped. 'We've got the body out, packed up ready to go. I'll send this with her to Doc in Adelaide and get the team to confirm, but this bookend was amongst the debris near the body, not behind the reception area like you'd expect.'

'So we are going with blunt force trauma as cause of death?' O'Connell pushed his glasses back up his nose as he sat down behind the desk, printed paperwork in hand.

'Too early to be sure, but I saw no sign of a knife or bullet wound. Other than the nails through her hands to keep her body in place, the only obvious injury was to the head.'

'We'll go with that for now and see what the Doc comes back with.'

'I'm done on the site now Sir. The other techs have turned up to help Penny. What do you need me to do?' Philips began removing the overalls as he opened the front counter pass-through and stepped around into the office area.

O'Connell turned his wrist to glance at his watch. 'Let's call it a day. Pick this all up Monday. We'll start with Con's business once they open, then we'll need to interview Marj. McGregor, you got pics of the bookend? Maybe she can say if it's one of hers or when it went missing?'

'There's no way Marj did this?' Philips placed his overalls in a bag and gave them to Penny for proper disposal.

'Same as there was no way Len Holmes covered up Tiffany Cox's murder.' O'Connell was only saying what Jenny knew to be true.

When she arrived in Coober Pedy, and Tiffany's body was found, it was Philips who found it difficult to believe a local, someone he grew up with or worked with could commit murder. It was she who told him to keep an open mind and she was right. Len's wife killed the young woman in a fit of jealousy and humiliation and Len covered it up.

But Marj, kill someone? It was her turn to face the fact, even the vivacious motel owner needed to be considered, questioned and officially eliminated from the suspect pool.

# Chapter 8

A crisp morning and clear sky promised sunshine. Fortunately, the temperatures were now in the mid-twenties Celsius instead of the summer scorching forty to fifty Jenny dealt with on arrival in the opal mining town.

Her mind wandered as she drove her rusty Dodge ute over the rough road. The lack of suspension left her neck stiff. The drive was quiet and contemplative as she focussed on the desert road. She couldn't wait to see Nick.

Out in the bush, community was everything. Nick was doing all he could to help rebuild the units at the pub. The same arsonist who burnt down Nick's Homestead also torched the weathered old fibro units the pub used to host visitors, and all to try to silence a witness.

The phantom smell of smoke tickled her nose whenever she thought about the fires. Her skin tingled with goose bumps even now. The corners of Jenny's mouth tipped up as the infamous rambling tin shed pub came into view. She shook off the memory of fire and focussed on Nick, his blue eyes, his reluctant smile.

Today she wanted to forget about a dead woman in Marj's office wall. Today she didn't even want to think about her missing cousin and aunt or Nick's dad's reopened murder case, or his missing mum. Today, she wanted to spend with Nick, all to herself.

It didn't matter what they did – drafting cattle, rebuilding the Homestead or maybe they could pack a picnic lunch and ride out to the Indigenous cave paintings where they could soak up the ancient, quiet, simple atmosphere together.

The parking area was deserted as she pulled up outside the pub. Two light aircraft were parked up alongside the road

31

like regular vehicles, but Jenny knew there was nothing ordinary about flying in to the remote location. Only the wealthy could afford to.

Apart from travelling tourists, the pub hosted the rich and famous from all over the world. Inside, it was a treasure trove of famous autographs, motor car memorabilia, and currency from every corner of the globe. It was what made the William Creek Pub so unique.

The Dodge door groaned as she pried it opened. Glancing up, she saw a figure strolling toward her, silhouetted against the early morning sun. His walk was unmistakable. Her insides fluttered like a schoolgirl as he stepped up to greet her.

He held a coffee cup in each hand and passed one to Jenny. 'I did a mental calculation when you sent the text you were leaving.' His smile was subtle, but even a slight grin was a welcome change from his usual cool expression. 'Figured you'd be here about now.'

'Perfect timing as always.' She stepped closer, reached for the cup in his hand, ignored the smell of her favourite brew and drew in the scent of his spicy aftershave.

'I missed you.' He leant forward, kissing her gently.

Butterflies thumped inside her stomach. She pulled away reluctantly. 'I missed you too.'

'Mrs B.'s on breakfast duty already. You hungry?'

'You know I'm always hungry.' She sipped her coffee, shoved the Dodge door shut with her foot and strolled with him, not bothering to lock the car. Everyone knew everyone out here.

'Did work go okay?'

'I'm not talking about work today. I'm here for fun and entertainment.' Nick lifted one eyebrow. The look was a mix of amusement and intrigue. Jenny blushed.

'How's the rebuild going?' She changed the subject. Although she stayed over in the Homestead on a few occasions before the fire, it was in one of the many guest bedrooms.

'I'll show you the accommodation after breakfast, then we can go out to the Homestead. It's coming along nicely. I think you'll like it.' Nick sounded as excited as Jenny felt.

Apart from helping to clean up after the fire, she hadn't been out to the property for weeks. A lot was happening while she was busy working in town and she missed the open space, helping with the stock on horseback and drinking billy tea with the jackaroos on breaks.

Nick held the door. Jenny glanced around the pub, with the low ceilings and clutter. It could easily have felt oppressive, but it was so different, so special. The atmosphere oozed personality. Rebecca, Mrs B.'s daughter tidied up behind the counter. The smell of bacon wafted in the air.

Jenny's stomach grumbled silently as she pulled out a stool at the front bar. 'Morning Rebecca.'

'Morning.' The publican's daughter worked part-time for Nick's station as an administrator. She and Nick shared history and at first, Jenny got a less than hospitable vibe from the woman, but the smile she offered on this occasion was warm and genuine. 'Long drive so early in the morning.'

'I needed the break. It's been a little crazy in town.'

'I heard. Is Marj alright?'

'Broken arm, but yes, she's recovering nicely.'

'What about the body?' Mrs B. appeared from the kitchen, two plates loaded high with bacon, baked beans, eggs and hash browns made Jenny's stomach grumble out loud. Mrs B. chuckled.

'You sound like Marj Mrs B., ready to make up some conspiratorial story about mass murderers or a cult.'

Mrs B. laughed loudly, the sound deep and resonating despite her tall, fine frame. 'Not at all luv. Just wondered if you knew who it was yet.'

'Nothing is confirmed. Waiting on DNA, dental records, that sort of thing. There'll be an official announcement once we know.'

'She's not working today Mrs B..' Nick retrieved a plate of food from Mrs B.'s hand as she put the other in front of Jenny.

'Sorry luv. I bet it's an occupational pain in the arse sometimes.'

'Local policing has its moments Mrs B..' Jenny watched the smile fall from the publican's face. 'What's up?'

'Luv…' she focused on her hands resting on the glossy wooden bar top and frowned, 'I should have said something.' Her eyes darted to Nick. 'To you, in particular Nick, years ago.'

Nick's fork stopped inches from his lips, fully loaded but going nowhere. 'What's up Mrs B.?'

'Nick told us last night about the police reopening his dad's suicide case as murder.'

The hairs on the back of Jenny's neck rose. She didn't want to do any of this today. She wanted a day to herself with Nick, no dead people, no missing people, but her stomach rolled and her body tightened. Her gut told her she needed to know this.

'Go on Mrs B.. It's okay. We often brush things aside at the time.' Jenny reached out, finding Mrs B.'s hand. She squeezed gently.

'That's it luv. That's exactly what I did. When the police said Ron committed suicide, it didn't make sense, but…' Her eyes pleaded with Nick. He wore the expression he always did when he didn't want anyone to know what he was thinking.

'Mum!' Rebecca pleaded for her to continue as her eyes darted from her mother to Nick and back.

'Sorry. I used to help out on occasion.' She stayed silent. Jenny's pulse kicked up a beat. She licked her lips and waited. 'Ron and Patricia,' she rubbed her hand over her face and up to smooth her hair. Her features contorted. 'They used to help runaways on occasion.'

'What sort of runaways?' Jenny heard her own voice like it was coming from someone else. Measured, careful, deep yet clear.

'I never asked questions luv. Ron and Patricia would ask me to do them a favour from time to time. Give one or two nights' accommodation here or there. That's all I ever did.'

'Like when my aunt and cousin stayed here?' The blood drained from Jenny's head. Little white sparkles played at the corners of her vision.

'The story I told you luv, was the one I was asked to tell if anyone ever came looking. I didn't know who they were to you at first.'

Nick reached for her as the room began to spin. 'I'm sorry luv. But I made a promise.' Mrs B. pleaded for Jenny to understand.

Her stomach bucked and rolled like a wild brumby, but there was nothing to hold down except half a cup of coffee.

'Jen. Listen to me.' She could hear Nick's voice coaxing her. 'Come outside. Get some fresh air.' She felt his arms tighten around her, physically lifting her from the stool, guiding her as she stumbled outside. The sound of her blood rushing from her head was all consuming.

# Chapter 9

Her dry-retching was muted against the pounding inside her head. 'I'm sorry,' she mumbled.

'Don't be ridiculous.' Nick squatted on his haunches next to her. 'Are you feeling okay now?'

'The horizon won't stay still, but yes, I don't think I'm going to puke if that's what you mean.'

'Take some more deep breaths.' Jenny stayed hunched over, crouched, with her head between her knees, willing herself not to barf, not to faint, to get her shit together.

'Mrs B. has known about Melanie and Aunt Carolyn all along. Nick, they ran away!' The shock was wearing off, to be replaced by a volatile mix of relief they might still be alive and outright anger they never let her know. *What were they running from?*

Something was niggling at her subconscious. Memories of her cousin fluttered through her mind like butterflies in spring, trying to tell her something, but the harder she focussed, the more fleeting the memory became.

'Come back inside.' Nick helped her to her feet. 'Let's get the whole story before you build your hopes up. I've seen you struggle with this for months Jenny.' He wrapped his arm around her, holding her to his chest.

His scent, and the gentle stroke of his hand on her back helped to slow her heartbeat. Part of her was embarrassed over losing her composure, the other part wanted to stay wrapped in Nick's strong embrace forever.

Pressing away from his chest, she told herself that coming to Coober Pedy wasn't a career move, it was a chance to find out what happened to her missing family. This was what she wanted. Now she needed to deal with it, no matter what.

Looking up, she focussed on Nick's clear blue eyes, creased with concern. 'I'm good.' She steadied her breathing. 'Let's do it.' Reluctantly she pulled free of the calmness of Nick's arms and strode back inside, chest out, head raised. The puzzle pieces were finally falling into place.

Mrs B. was on the customer's side of the bar, chewing her thumb nail when Jenny returned. 'I'm so sorry luv,' she said again. Jenny held her hand up.

'It's alright Mrs B. I understand you didn't know who you could tell. Did my cousin or aunt ever say anything to you about why they were running?'

'No luv. I barely saw them. Ron picked them up from here and drove them to William Creek Station.'

'So Ed was right.' Jenny turned to Nick. 'He *did* see Mel at your place.' Jenny's pulse kicked up a gear. This time, there would be no near-fainting spells.

'You found her handwriting in the accounts ledger. We always knew there was a good chance she stayed. Now we understand why. That weird book of coded information might be connected.' Nick pulled a stool out, sat and picked up his cutlery ready to get back to his breakfast.

'I saw it when you brought it in.' Mrs B. accepted the cup of tea Rebecca offered her. 'I can't be sure, but Ron and Patricia must have kept some type of record of the people they helped. Maybe someone came looking for a runaway and killed Nick's dad out of rage?'

Mrs B. was beginning to sound like Marj and her murder theories after all, but her reasoning was sound. 'It certainly sheds a new light on the ledger Nick. We should probably take it in to Sarge and O'Connell to see if we can decipher it.'

'It's all yours. If it helps find out who killed dad and where mum is, then I'm all for it. It could have information on where your family went after the station too. If we can figure it out.'

Jenny pictured the columns in her head. Nothing made any sense. There was no clear date format, no names, no locations she could recognise. 'Where is it?'

'It's here. I left it with Rebecca the night of the fire,' he pointed with his knife, 'and then I didn't want to store it in the workman's quarters. I was worried it might get damaged or lost.'

'I'll grab it.' Rebecca rushed through the swinging doors leading to the kitchen.

As much as Jenny planned to leave all the murder and mayhem behind her this weekend, the idea Melanie might be alive and they could find details in the ledger from William Creek Station was too much of a lure to ignore.

'Nick, are you okay if we take a look now?' Jenny lifted her eyebrows, her voice a whisper.

'If it has anything to do with dad, we need to check it over before we give it to your boss, so I'm in.'

Rebecca rushed back into the bar breathless. Her usually neat and tidy mousey-brown ponytail was loose, with pieces of hair dangling around her earlobes.

'Are you two going to look at this now?' Jenny nodded as Rebecca handed it over. 'Do you mind if I help?'

'Of course not.' Jenny opened the hard-backed accounts ledger and began peering at the details. There were no column headings on any of the pages. She flicked past ten, twenty pages then turned to face Nick. 'Did you ever notice the coming and going of these people?'

Nick sighed. 'No, but I went to boarding school in year nine. Before that, I was too absorbed in doing what farm boys do, to notice strange girls or anyone out of the ordinary. We took tourists out trail riding all the time. Backpackers and travelling jackaroos came and went all year…' He trailed off, his expression a mix of frustration and helplessness.

She reached for his hand and squeezed. 'I get it. Honestly. My cousin and aunt ran away from home and I have no idea why.'

# Chapter 10

The motel crime scene was full of high-vis clothing and forensic techs. The scene appeared more like an alien landing investigation. With full length disposable overalls, goggles, gloves and evidence bags in hand, Jenny couldn't help but feel like she was on the site of a chemical spill, not a vehicle accident.

'Hey Penny.' Jenny waited outside the police tape for the scientist to come to her.

'What's up?'

She wiggled a cappuccino cup in the air. Penny was as big a coffee snob as Jenny, except unlike her, Penny didn't like caramel syrup in her espresso.

Penny ducked under the tape. 'You-are-a-life saver!' She reached for the coffee.

'All part of the service.' They sipped their coffee in comfortable silence a moment. 'Looks like we got a hit on the dental records. Can you get Doc to put a rush on checking them against the victim for an ID?'

'That was fast.' Penny glanced at her watch. How did you find out so quickly?

'Turns out, Franny Kovac visited a dentist locally when she was younger, and when she was here five years ago. First thing this morning they saw the email I sent out Saturday, and they rang.'

'Brilliant. I'll make a call.' She sculled the rest of her coffee and handed Jenny the empty. 'It's not what you know but who you know.' Penny flashed a mischievous look.

'How is it you get Doc to jump through hoops anyway?' Jenny slowly finished her coffee, savouring it to the last drop.

'I dated his son at Uni.'

'Oh. Wouldn't that normally be a bad thing? Breaking up with the guy, then working with his dad?'

'Doc's pretty straight-up. A no-nonsense type of guy. After all, he does talk to dead people all day.'

They giggled. 'How's Nick doing?'

'Rebuild is coming along. We managed to squeeze in a picnic, out by the Indigenous artworks I told you about.' Her skin tingled at the thought of the escarpment, the cool cave with traditional paintings dating back thousands of years, the winding lower valley full of lush green grass – a stark contrast against the surrounding desert.

'Do tell.' Her cheeks must have been flushing.

'Nothing to tell.'

'Oh my god woman. Get the man into bed before you both burst.' Jenny slapped her friend's arm gently.

'I'll see you for lunch.' Jenny changed the subject. 'I've got news. *Big* news about my cousin and aunt.'

'You can't do that to me,' Penny pouted. 'I might not even have time for a lunch break.'

'You better make time then.' Jenny waved as she strolled away leaving Penny open mouthed.

Two minutes of brisk walking down the road and she was back inside the police station, wondering how the scorching hot summer suddenly turned to cool mornings.

'Sarge in yet?' Jenny peered through the open doorway at the back of the office area.

'On his way. What you got Williams?' O'Connell accepted the coffee she offered, nodding his thanks.

'I found something that might help with Nick's dad's case. I also wanted to talk to him about how he went with Murphy.'

'No time this morning. You and Philips need to interview Con and his team, then bring Marj in for questioning.'

'Can't we interview Marj at the motel?'

'You said it yourself when you arrived in town Williams. You have to keep an open mind and do everything by the book.'

He was right. As much as Jenny loved Marj, the woman knew the victim and witnesses saw them arguing shortly before Franny died. Sighing, she placed Philips' coffee on the front counter before dawdling over to her locker.

After putting her backpack away, she pulled on her utility vest, strapped on the waist belt with her weapon holster and crossed over to the gun safe to log out her duty weapon.

As she pushed the safe closed, Philips entered the station.

'We are out and about today partner. Let's go, I'll drive, you drink.' She pointed to the coffee on the front counter.

# Chapter 11

The police Landcruiser rode rough over the poorly maintained bitumen road. Jenny spotted discarded opal mullock in hues of white and red scattered across the horizon as they drove past rundown houses with barren gardens on the outskirts of town. Residential buildings gave way to scattered commercial allotments featuring huge sheds, chain fences and more dry, red dirt.

Jenny guided the four-wheel drive into a dusty yard. On one side, piles of gravel and sand separated by concrete walls lined up against a tall, ring fence. At the opposite end to the entry, she could see a tower, with a hopper below. A cement truck parked beneath, filling up to deliver a load.

The site office consisted of two transportable buildings jammed either side an aluminium ramp, a separate ablution block was set back between the offices. A large, faded blue and yellow sign announced *Papa Construction*.

'Neat set up. He's got all the bases covered here. Does Con tender for all the highway and building work in town or does he just get it by default?' Jenny turned the motor off, checked her service weapon holster was clipped closed and opened the driver's door.

'No idea. Maybe we should ask?' Philips slammed the passenger side door. They strolled up the ramp, stopping at the sound of raised voices. Jenny resisted the urge to put her hand on her weapon. A few seconds of taking in the tone, made it clear it was likely a family fight.

Working with your partner could be challenging. Her mum and dad used to have massive rows from time to time, but they always made up. Thinking about her parents reminded her of Melanie, running away. She planned to ring her mum and dad tonight to tell them the news.

Jenny entered the office, Philips a step behind. As expected, the transportable office boasted commercial fake timber linoleum flooring, a chipped wooden veneer reception desk which clashed with the floor and two black uncomfortable looking plastic moulded reception chairs.

Mr and Mrs Papadakis turned at the sight of her uniform. Mrs Papadakis's eyes drifted to Jenny's weapon, then up to her face. The woman's eyes grew wide, but her expression flattened quickly.

'What can we do for you officers?' Con Papadakis plastered a well-practised smile on his face, but his rapidly rising chest and flushed cheeks told a different story.

'I'm Constable Williams. I'm sure you know Constable Philips.' Con nodded. Philips took his Akubra off and dropped his head toward Mrs Papadakis.

'We are here to ask you a few questions about the repair work done on the Opal Inn Motel approximately five years back.' Jenny continued as Philips retrieved a notepad from his top pocket.

Con frowned, studying Philips a moment, then diverted his eyes back to Jenny. 'What do you need?'

'Firstly, we'd like to confirm you conducted the repairs to Marj's office.' Con nodded. 'Do you have the work schedule from the job?'

Con turned to Mrs Papadakis, who remained motionless. Jenny's curiosity piqued. Was this embarrassment about being caught fighting or was it something else? Silence hung as Jenny and Philips waited.

'Mum…' A tall, olive-skinned woman in her mid-twenties wandered into the office, stopping when she spotted two officers standing in the foyer. She glanced from Jenny to

Con. 'Ah sorry. I can come back in a minute.' She began to back up, but Con waved a hand at her.

'Tina. Hang on a sec. I need you to pull a job from our files.' The woman waited without saying a word. 'We did a repair on the reception area at the Opal Inn Motel in late twenty-ten. Can you grab the file?

Jenny did a quick calculation. Not quite five years but the timing was close enough. Something was bugging her. Neither Con nor his wife asked why they wanted the file. Did they know about the body already? Coober Pedy was a small town. News travelled at lightning speed, especially when the word *murder* was uttered.

'Okay.' The woman disappeared back the way she came in.

'What's this about?' Con's tone was casual as he strode around the reception desk. Mrs Papadakis retreated to a workstation at the furthest end of the office. Her eyes continued to glance over as Con waited for an answer.

'I'll need to see the records first. Then I can explain.'

'Now look here. I have a right to know why you want to look through my records.' Con puffed up his chest.

'Con. She's new. It's okay mate. It's just a routine check. You heard about the accident. Right?' Con nodded at Philips. Jenny didn't like pussy-footing around the subject, but Philips was right. Con could easily ask for a warrant and not cooperate. But then, if he did, he could implicate himself in a murder.

'Here it is dad.' Jenny forced her expression to remain neutral as she studied the young woman. Tina was only a few inches shorter than Jenny's six foot, while her parents were barely five foot six. Her hair was light brown, eyes green or hazel, build slighter. Her olive skin was where any similarity to Con or his wife stopped.

Holding out a manila folder to Con, she considered Jenny's focussed gaze, but averted her eyes quickly when Jenny stepped forward to retrieve the file. Instead of handing over cooperatively, Con held it to his chest, arms wrapped around it tightly like a spoiled child with a teddy bear.

'Now. Will you tell me what this is about?'

Jenny puffed out a breath. 'The body of a woman was found in the wreckage after the accident Mr Papadakis.' He waited, a crease on his brow told her he might not have any idea about the victim after all.

'Sir. The woman was encased in the walls of the rebuild.' She held back the details about the nailed hands and the possible ID of the victim.

The daughter and Con sucked in a sharp breath simultaneously. Jenny glanced at Mrs Papadakis. Her eyes were looking at a ledger on the desk. Was she not listening, pretending not to listen or unaffected by the news?

'That's horrible.' The daughter's voice was high pitched.

'I'm sorry to hear that.' Con held the file out in front of him, waving it in the air as though it was suddenly a venomous snake. 'I assure you Constable, this has nothing to do with my family or any of my workers.'

'We appreciate your cooperation Mr Papadakis, if you could also provide details of all the tradesmen who accessed the site from framing to plasterboard.'

'Did you hear what he said?' Jenny jumped as Mrs Papadakis spoke. The woman was a ghost, having travelled from the desk twenty metres away to the reception area without being noticed.

'We heard Mrs Papadakis, but we have a job to do. The woman didn't get trapped behind the plasterboard and paint by herself. Someone put her there.'

The daughter gasped, wavering as though she might faint. Philips stepped in before Con could do anything. 'Take a seat Tina.' Philips motioned for Con to grab a chair. Mr Papadakis rushed around the counter, grabbed a chair on wheels and rolled it at full speed up to his daughter. Holding it, he waited for her to sit, steadying the chair as she did, before letting go.

'Do you know who the victim is yet?' Con rubbed his balding crown.

'We are waiting for a formal ID, but we believe we've identified her.' Jenny didn't see any reason to hold back the sex of the victim. She watched each face carefully. Con's mouth hung open. Tina's eyes were wide and on the verge of tears, while Mrs Papadakis stared blankly at the file in Jenny's hand.

'We'll take this and be in touch if we have any more questions. We *will* need to interview any staff who worked on the project.' Jenny kept her eyes on Con. He nodded slowly, his eyes darting to his daughter frequently.

'Thanks for this.' Philips held his hand out. Con shook it automatically. Philips turned to Tina, his eyes anxious. 'You okay?' She nodded. He didn't look convinced, but Jenny couldn't help wondering over the dramatic display.

'Let's go Philips.' Jenny tucked the file under her arm and turned to leave. Philips jogged up behind her halfway down the ramp.

'That was a bit callous.' He spoke over her shoulder. 'The Papadakises were accommodating.'

'Philips. Someone killed a woman, nailed her to the frames and hid her in a wall. If Mrs Barton hadn't driven her car into Marj's reception area, our victim would have remained missing forever. No one would know where she was.

Jenny's emotions were rising rapidly. She knew this was about Melanie and the news she may be alive and deliberately remaining hidden for nearly ten years.

'The Papadakis family have been here all my life Jenny.' The use of her first name only proved he was not holding these suspects at arm's length. Like her first case in town, when Philips didn't want to believe a local killed someone.

'Philips. Like I said. Our victim didn't get into that wall on her own. Someone put her there. Someone in that room,' she swung around and pointed as she opened the driver's side door of the Landcruiser, 'could have been involved. They organised the tradies.'

'It's probably just a tradesman travelling through. Someone out of work from the mines. Or a backpacker helping out.'

Jenny slipped behind the wheel, shaking her head. Denial was a dangerous thing, but small towns always struggled to point the finger at anyone they knew. Someone they grew up with.

'We'll go over the files. See who worked on the job. We have to stay impartial Philips.'

He pouted. She could see he knew she was right, but at the same time, Danny Philips was a local. Moved here when he was very young. This was the only place he knew. A desolate, mining town full of people wanting to distance themselves from the rest of the world.

'I hope you're right Danny.' She used his first name to soften her words more. 'But remember Tiffany. Remember even those people we love can be capable of horrible things.'

Philips was devastated when it turned out his friend and former Senior Constable had covered up the local girl's murder. She started the car as he put his seatbelt on, but her mind was drifting to Marj. Could she keep an open mind with the bright, loving woman who befriended her the day she arrived?

She was about to find out.

# Chapter 12

Jenny's stomach knotted as Marj sipped from the bottle of water she offered her. Local policing had never felt difficult, until today.

'Sorry to bring you in here Marj, but we need to tape the interview. You understand?' Marj's dimples popped to life.

'You do what you have to do luv.' She twisted the lid back on the water bottle and thumped it down on the table. 'I didn't kill Franny. You need to find the mongrel who did.' Jutting out her chin, she sat back and folded her arms over her chest.

'Okay. Ready?' Marj nodded. Jenny tipped her head for Philips to turn the recording equipment on.

'Can you state your name for the record.' Marj did. 'We are still waiting on confirmation, but we believe the body found in the wall of your office, was that of Franny Kovac so for the purposes of this interview, we'll be referring to her as *the victim*. Do you understand?' Another nod.

'Can you answer for the recording please.'

'Yes luv.'

Jenny grinned. There was no point asking Marj to use her official title. It was never going to happen. She continued with the formalities.

'What was your relationship to the victim?'

'Franny was my de-facto, Jason Kovac's sister.'

'Did you know her well?' These were baseline questions used in any suspect questioning to set the interviewee at ease and for the interviewer to get a feel for what a lie might look like. Jenny's heart ached at having to do this to Marj.

'I moved in with Jason in my mid-twenties. I didn't meet Franny until nearly ten years later. Franny only ever turned up when she wanted something from Jason.'

'So you didn't get along?'

Jenny couldn't help but wish Marj brought a lawyer with her. Stan called one, but Marj obviously didn't want one to attend. As much as she wanted to go easy on the motel owner, she knew she couldn't. The Coober Pedy police didn't need another rough job like Len's case. Or Nick's dad's case. Or her own family disappearance. So many critical cases were mismanaged in this town.

Jenny knew Sergeant Mackenzie was supposed to be in charge at the time, but he was grief-stricken after the accidental death of his daughter. When Jenny got to town, she would have been ready to rat the man out for dropping the ball on these cases. He was hard on her, making her life almost unbearable in those first months, but now. Now she felt like it was her duty to protect him.

'I didn't think much of Franny. Don't get me wrong, on the surface, she was a laugh a minute, but she was a shallow soul. No one *really* liked Franny, not once they got to know her.'

'When was the last time you recall seeing the victim?'

Marj picked at the edge of her lip. 'Jason died on the twenty first of September twenty ten. The funeral was held five days later. Franny didn't come. But she turned up two days later for the reading of the Will.'

'So the reading was the last time you saw her?'

'The evening after that. We had a big, loud fight in the middle of the dining room. Half the bloody town saw it. She was all riled up about being left out of the will. Threatened to bring in some fancy city lawyer to get her share.'

*Where was a lawyer when you needed one!* Jenny glanced at Philips, taking notes, his eyebrows raised. She sighed.

'You had motive to kill the victim Marj.' Jenny kept her voice calm.

'Yep. Certainly did, but if I killed everyone who pissed me off, there wouldn't be enough walls in my office to fit them all.'

Philips chuckled. Jenny's stomach knotted. Marj wasn't helping her case, but deep down Jenny knew there was no way she killed her sister-in-law. Now she just needed to prove it.

'You said no-one liked the victim. Can you think of anyone specific? Anyone who might like to see her dead?'

'Look. Franny flew in and out of Coober Pedy like a stealthy fart. She'd arrive all nice, looking like butter wouldn't melt in her mouth, but by the time she left town, all hell would have broken loose. Franny was a looker. Tall, thin, green eyes, auburn hair.' Marj grinned. 'A little bit like you come to think of it.' She chuckled. 'But you're nothing like her luv. Franny lured men in like a black widow spider. Just when they thought they were on cloud nine, she'd suck the life out of them.'

'Any man in particular?' Jenny leant forward. Sex, broken hearts, jealous wives. They were all excellent motives for murder.

Marj rolled her lips together, as though she wanted to take back her last few words. She shook her head, a little too rigorously.

'No luv. Not that I know anything about.'

Marj was the gossip queen of the entire town. She knew everything about everybody. Hell, she often knew things the police were working on before they announced them, like her last case, when a purse went missing from the crime scene and turned up outside the dumpster at the rear of the motel.

Marj called the police, fully aware they were looking for it, but well before they issued any sort of statement or canvassed local businesses. She was a veritable opal mine of local gossip.

'Who are you protecting Marj?'

She shook her head gently. 'No one in particular. Like I said, Franny played up with quite a few local boys. Some were married. No need to drag it all up now.'

'Marj. When I got here, I investigated the Tiffany Cox murder. You remember right?' Marj nodded like she knew where Jenny was leading her. 'Tiffany was killed by a jealous wife.' Another nod. 'If Franny slept around with whoever she wanted, then one of those guy's wives, or girlfriends could have killed Franny. You're our only suspect Marj. Tell us what you know so we can clear your name, and find the person who did this.'

Marj leant back in her seat, folded her arms across her chest and said nothing. Not one little word.

# Chapter 13

O'Connell pulled his reading glass off and placed them on the table. Rubbing the bridge of his nose, he sighed. 'We could hold her, for impeding a police investigation.'

'She's not talking Sir.'

'We've got no evidence she has anything to do with the murder.' Philips crossed his arms and leant against the front counter, watching the Senior Constable – waiting.

'I agree. It's all circumstantial.' Sarge rolled a clean whiteboard toward O'Connell's desk. 'Let's get this updated.' He tapped the top of the board. 'Did Marj recognise the possible murder weapon?'

'Yes Sir. She said the matching bookend was still in her office and she wondered where its pair had gone, but assumed it was likely broken in the last crash.'

'Let her go home. We'll go over the records from the builder this afternoon. Make a list of all the tradesmen who worked on the job.' He turned to leave but stopped.

'Williams, O'Connell tells me you've got some fresh information on Ron Johnston's case.'

Jenny glanced at O'Connell, then nodded. 'Yes Sarge.'

'Bring it to my office. I spoke to Kent Murphy the other week, then again Saturday. I'll update you.'

Why did he keep his meeting with Kent from her? She wanted to make a fuss, but bit her tongue. The last few months had been much more civil between them. She didn't want to ruin it by getting upset now.

Jenny rushed to her locker, removed the ledger then stopped. O'Connell was watching her when she turned around. She glanced around to see Philips stepping out of the main office area. 'I'm going to have to tell him about Melanie and Aunt Carolyn.'

'I know.' O'Connell put his readers back on, the corners of his mouth tilted upward.

'It's not funny,' she whispered.

'I think you'll find it is.' She gaped at him, shook her head, slammed the door of her locker and stomped toward Sarge's office.

Had O'Connell already told her boss about her personal agenda? Jenny stopped outside the door to knock. As her hand rose, Sarge called out. 'Just come in Williams.'

'Yes Sir.' She scampered toward his desk, placing the open ledger down in front of him.

He leant forward from his reclined position in the high-backed office chair. 'What's this?'

'We found it a few months back in Nick's family cellar. Before the fire. It's a ledger, with strange coded input.'

'How is this related to Ron Johnston's death?'

'I was chatting with Mrs B. on Sunday. She told me Ron and Patricia used to help relocate runaways.'

Sarge whistled. 'Sly old bird. She's kept that to herself a while.'

'Mrs B. didn't think it was relevant, until we re-opened Nick's dad's case and reclassified it as murder.'

'And you think these runaway relocations might have something to do with Ron's murder?'

'It might provide motive Sir.'

Sarge pursed his lips. Jenny fidgeted. Was he going to tell her what Murphy knew about Patricia? The day Nick was shot, the station owner said he was a tough nut, like his mum. Which made Jenny believe he knew Nick's mum intimately.

Nick shared his suspicions about Kent and Patricia possibly having an affair before she went missing. But now she knew what the Johnston family were doing, it was more likely Mr Murphy knew something about it.

'I didn't get much out of Kent the other week, but he contacted me when he heard we were investigating Ron's murder. That's why I went back out to see him Saturday. It seems there was a little network aiding the Johnston's in their relocation program.' Sarge tapped his fingers on his desk, his eyes focussed on her, waiting for something. She swallowed hard.

'Sir.' Her voice was unsure.

'Yes?'

'I kind of need to tell you something else.' He waited, his fingers still tapping. 'The ledger, Nick found. It might help with another cold case.'

The corners of Sergeant Mackenzie's mouth lifted. He forced them back into a stern, deadpan look. 'And?'

'Ron's death, Patricia's disappearance. I think they are linked.' He stopped tapping his fingers, relaxed back into the vinyl office chair and crossed his hands in his lap.

Drops of sweat popped up on Jenny's back, despite the cooler day. 'Mrs B. recognised my cousin and aunt amongst the people Ron and Patricia helped relocate.'

He watched her silently. She squirmed under his gaze. 'That was hard. Wasn't it?'

Jenny opened her mouth to speak, but closed it again. He had no idea how hard it was.

'I did a background check on you before you came Williams. I must admit, I missed the cold case about your aunt and cousin at first, but then I started thinking. I said to myself, *she's driven. Wired harder than normal. Something isn't quite right.* So I dug some more.'

'I wanted to tell you Sir, but you and I.'

'Didn't get off on the right foot.' He finished her sentence.

She nodded.

'Well, it's time to put the cards on the table. When Murphy called, he told me about Patricia's soft spot for domestic violence victims. Apparently, her dad came back from the war broken. He drank too much and used to smack her mum around.'

Jenny gasped. Nick never mentioned anything about a granddad. Did he know? A sudden thought kicked her in the stomach. Nausea swept over her. She'd linked runaways with Ron and Patricia, but there was simply no way Melanie and Aunt Carolyn were at William Creek Station to escape domestic violence. Just no way. *Was there?*

# Chapter 14

A pile of papers was strewn all over the office counter. 'Clive Watson was the plasterer. It makes sense we start with him.' Jenny turned to Philips, lifted up an invoice and placed it on a pile alongside her partner.

'I'll see if these contact details are current.' He tapped keys on the main office computer.

'Run him for a police record while you're there.' Jenny flipped through invoices, making sure not to miss any other tradies who might have been on the scene before the plasterboard was fitted.

'There's also the chippy. Do plasterers or carpenters fit insulation? What about the plastic wrap?' Jenny quizzed Philips. His eyebrows knitted together as his shoulders shrugged.

'Don't ask me. I'm a cop, not a tradie for a reason.'

'Well the carpenter was also a contractor, but it looks like he did a lot of work for the Papadakis family.'

'What's his name?' Philips kept tapping keys.

'Tom Hammond.'

'Any contact info?'

'Nothing on here. Can you do a local licence check for his name while you're there?'

'Will do.'

'You two. Time to call it a day.' O'Connell rose from his desk. 'We'll contact the tradesmen tomorrow. Do the interviews then.'

'We've not finished compiling the list yet Sir.' Jenny held her ground, but Philips was already moving toward his locker. He didn't need to be told twice to knock off. Jenny envied him at times. Married, with a four-year-old at home, Philips was a settled guy. Content being a local cop.

Jenny's unsolved family case wasn't the only reason she was discontent. Ever since Melanie went missing, she aspired to be a cop, but now, after working on the last few cases, and meeting detectives from Adelaide, she felt driven to rise up the ranks in the police force. Not only to solve Melanie and Aunt Carolyn's disappearance, but to be able to give closure to so many other people in her situation.

The loved ones of every missing person – every murder victim, deserved answers. They deserved to know the circumstances surrounding the case. And the more she worked on major crimes, the more she desperately wanted to find closure for others.

'They aren't going anywhere today Williams and we all have to eat.' O'Connell powered down his computer and directed her to do the same. 'It's an order.'

'Yes Sir.' Jenny nodded, piled up the paperwork spread all over the bench and crossed the room to stow it away in a locked cabinet.

'I'm sure even McGregor has knocked off by now. Grab a beer with her. Catch up. Let your hair down.'

'I will Sir.'

O'Connell lifted the countertop, turned and waited to make sure Jenny did indeed grab her bag from her locker. 'Lock up Philips. Make sure she doesn't stay in here.'

Philips grinned, mock saluted and steered Jenny toward the exit. 'Come on Williams. I'll come over for a drink too. The volunteers have been busy cleaning up the accident scene. Dianna is bringing Tommy in for dinner. You can practise your signing.'

Jenny relaxed. Since moving to the opal mining town, she'd made a few friends, including Danny's wife Dianna. Her lip-reading was exceptional, but Jenny wanted to be able to converse with her in her own sign language. It was hard, but she was slowly getting the hang of it.

'Okay. You've twisted my arm. Let's go.'

Five minutes later, still in uniform, they wandered into the main dining area. A swarm of orange and yellow high-vis lined the long timber bar, with Penny, telling stories, hands flying around in all directions, right in the centre of the mass.

Jenny tingled on the inside. Penny was confident, focussed and uncompromising. The trait made her think of Melanie, who always appeared to be the same on the outside. But if she was hiding from domestic violence at home…Jenny shook her head to clear the thought. Now wasn't the time to rehash what Melanie might have run away from.

'Hey. Beer for my friend.' Penny spotted Jenny and waved, then returned to her story-telling undeterred.

Stan chuckled from behind the bar, picked up a chilled glass from the tray and pulled a cold beer from the bar tap. It was on the mat, with a frothing head spilling over before Jenny reached it.

'First one's on the house. Marj's orders.' He nodded to the woman sitting at the far end of the room.

Jenny lifted the beer in salute, then drank deeply. Seeing Marj in the bar this early was strange, but with a smashed-up office, there was no need to man reception until her usual closing time.

'How's she going?' Jenny leant forward so Stan could hear over the din of voices, mostly Penny's, all around her.

'She's sad Franny's gone for good, but she's being cagey too.'

'Cagey how?'

'I don't know. I don't want to get her into any trouble. I wouldn't say anything, but I know I can trust you.' Jenny nodded. 'I know she didn't kill Franny, but she might know who would make a good suspect.'

'I got that impression when we interviewed her today. Let me know if you think she's in danger.'

Stan gave a scout's salute, picked up a clean cloth and busied himself polishing glasses.

'Hey. No shop talk. Drink.' Penny nudged her shoulder.

'I'm starving. Let's grab a seat.' Jenny stepped away from the bar, then turned to make sure Penny was joining her.

The scientist put a finger in the air to indicate she needed a second, then continued to finish her story. Jenny sipped her beer, crossed the room and pulled out a chair at one of the long tables in the middle of the dining area. As she slid into the seat, she heard a round of laughter peal from the bar flies hanging around Penny.

'She certainly knows how to hold a room.' Philips slid into a seat alongside her, beer in hand.

'That's for sure.' Across from their table, Jenny noticed Marj take a seat at a smaller round table with Tina Papadakis. 'How well do you know Tina? Is she married?' She lifted her beer toward the pair.

'Not well. She's quite a few years younger than me. I don't think she's married. She still uses her dad's last name. I've seen her in here a few times, but not for ages. Not since Jason died.'

'What's Jason got to do with Tina?'

'Jason Kovac was Tina's godfather.'

'Was Marj her godmother?'

'Don't think so. Maybe? You'll have to ask I guess. Does it matter?'

Jenny gulped a mouthful of her beer, slid the glass aside and scanned the menu she knew by heart. 'Probably not.'

'Time to party.' Penny sat down, blocking Jenny's view of Marj and Tina. 'Brought you another one.'

'I'm not doing Karaoke Penny.'

'Not even if Nev and Tim join in?' Penny pointed to the doorway.

Jenny turned to see her roommates waving. Like Penny, the boys were ex-med students and were always keen for a party. None of them appeared to have an *off* switch.

Promising herself she'd leave early, Jenny reached for the beer in Penny's hand. 'I haven't finished my first one and I need food before I drink this.'

'Well let's order then.' Penny pushed up from the table. Jenny joined her.

'Did you find anything useful today?' Jenny's question was cut short by the new waitress, ready and waiting at the counter to take their order.

'What can I get you officer?' The woman's expression was calm against the rowdy atmosphere.

'Kelly, isn't it?' Jenny asked, she nodded, not wanting to draw the conversation out. From all accounts, that was nothing unusual. Cheryl said she was quiet.

'I'll grab the chicken parmigiana. What are you having Penny?'

'Steak. I need red meat. Lugging debris all over the place is hard work, even with these guys helping.' She hoicked a thumb at the sea of CFS and SES volunteers.

They paid, then turned, chatting as they wove their way back to their table. 'Where's the rest of your team?'

Penny shrugged. 'They're on their way back to Adelaide. With the extra hands, we isolated the area where the body was and got all the debris cleaned out today.'

'So you head home tomorrow too?'

'No. I've got a few more days here finishing up. Making sure nothing was missed, but the bulk of the work is done.'

They slid into their seats. Penny placed the order buzzer on the table and picked up her white wine in one smooth motion.

Jenny reached for her beer as Dianna and Tommy joined Philips. The boy's blonde hair bounced when he jumped on his dad for a hug. Spotting her, he waved over his dad's shoulder. Jenny smiled, waved back, then turned to greet Nev and Tim. She opened her mouth to speak, but stopped as something caught her eye.

Tina rose from the table abruptly enough to nearly knock her chair over. Marj jumped up, placing her hand on Tina's arm which she vigorously slapped away, before storming from the motel restaurant without a backward glance.

# Chapter 15

The sun was long set by the time Jenny pried herself out of the motel. The last few days left her lacking in energy but she knew the cause. Finding out Melanie probably ran away from home, tormented Jenny deep in her spirit.

The door to the dugout she shared with Tim and Nev creaked as she pushed it open. Coober Pedy was known for the cave-like homes many of the miners carved out of the rock while searching for their fortune in opals. But Jenny knew most were dank, dark caverns with broken windows and old farm gates for doors.

She was lucky to have found a place like this one. Deep, circular tool marks and narrow drill holes left no doubt it was once a working mine, but now it was a permanent rental house for the South Australian Health Department. The boys were employed by SA Health, and she was lucky to have been invited by Tim and Nev to stay in the quaint little home.

Tastefully decorated with old cottage style furniture and fittings, it made her comfortable with its homely vibe, but tonight the atmosphere did nothing to stop her gut from cramping. Glancing at her watch, she made up her mind it was time to update her parents with her news about Aunt Carolyn and Melanie.

Not bothering to close her door, she put her backpack on the dresser and turned to view the full height antique mirror she used as her investigation board. Reaching out, she touched the postcard Melanie sent from Coober Pedy nearly ten years ago. They were going on a holiday, at least that's what she was told.

Now, as she studied the postcard with her latest piece of information about Ron and Patricia's relocation program in mind, she could see the code behind the words.

*Maybe we'll get to ride horses and stay at William Creek Station, but I'm going to really miss you Jen xoxo!*

Jenny gently slid the postcard back into the mirror frame and flopped onto her bed, fighting the urge to let loose the hot tears burning behind her eyes. They stayed buried. She was too angry for tears.

Jumping up from the soft bed, she grabbed her phone from her bag and wandered outside to find a mobile network signal.

The backlit screen glowed in the pitch-black night beyond the dugout. Dialling, she waited, the phone at her ear, her eyes staring up at the billions of stars twinkling in the night sky. Coober Pedy was out in the middle of nowhere, literally, and the Milky Way, the Southern Cross, the awesome array of the heavens shone down out here like nothing she'd ever seen in her life.

'Jenny. How are you?' Her mum's voice made her heart skip a beat. She never missed her mum until she heard her voice. Hot tears sprung to life.

'Mum.' Her voiced croaked. 'How are you?'

'What's up bub? Has your new man upset you already?'

'No mum. I'm good. There's been a breakthrough in Melanie and Aunt Carolyn's case.' Silence greeted her. 'Mum?' She pulled the phone away from her ear, checked the reception. *Three bars, all good.* 'Mum?'

'I'm here Jenny.' The nickname was gone. At least she wasn't calling her Jennifer. That always meant she was in trouble. 'Let me get your dad.'

'If you…' She heard the phone rattle as her mum put it down on the hardwood antique side-table below the ancient turn-dial wall phone her dad refused to replace. *Telstra provides it for free, what do I need one of those new push button jobs for?*

She shook her head, trying to find the funny side, but her stomach was rolling and bucking. Why did she have to talk to dad about this? She knew he didn't want her digging into Melanie's disappearance. She wanted to tell her mum, so she could tell him. It was the way things were done in her family. No one ever tried to talk dad into anything head on. It was a slow, manipulative process her mum was exceptionally skilled at. Why wasn't she convincing him this time?

'Jennifer?' *Damn.*

'Hey dad. Mum told you about the news then?'

'You know you shouldn't be digging around in this.'

'No. I don't dad,' she blurted out. 'I didn't call to argue.' Telling herself to calm down, she tried again. 'I called to tell you we now know Melanie and Aunt Carolyn likely stayed at the William Creek Station while they were here.'

'We knew that.'

'Yes, but what we didn't know was that Nick's mum and dad used to help runaways relocate.'

'Nick's mum and dad?'

Jenny rolled her eyes. 'Yes, you know the guy I'm seeing. The William Creek Station owner?' The nervous rash she got when her emotions ran high began to rise over her chest and neck like a roaring fire.

'Jennifer. You need to leave this alone. It will only end in tears for you girly.' Jenny opened her mouth to reply, but stopped as her mind raced through her dad's words again. Did he already know why Melanie ran away?

'You knew they ran away.' The snappy words were out of her mouth before she could stop them.

'I'm not discussing this with you Jennifer.'

'Well you might have to dad. We've officially reopened Nick's dad's death as a murder investigation and we'll be questioning the known relatives of *absolutely everyone* Ron and Patricia Johnston helped relocate.' Her hands shook. Her voice quavered. Her head thumped like it was about to explode. There was no containing her rage as she continued to rant.

'You might not want to talk to me, but at some point, you might not have a choice.'

'I told you not to go up there.'

'Yeah, why was that dad? Since you seem to have known all along they left by choice, you must know why. *Why dad?* Why did Melanie and Aunt Carolyn *run away*!' She heard herself yelling now, like her rational mind was hovering over the scene. Shaking with rage, she struggled to hold the phone steady.

'Get a badge and all of a sudden some crazy police investigation rots your bloody brain. Leave it alone Jenny. It's family business.' The phone line went dead.

Jenny gaped at the phone screen, her heart thumping in her chest like she'd run a marathon. Her ears rang with rushing blood. 'Get yourself together.' She drew a deep, lung full of air and let it out slowly. Her hands wouldn't stop shaking.

There was no doubt in her mind now. Her family must know why Melanie and Aunt Carolyn left. But why keep it a secret from her all this time? Was she so oblivious back then? Probably. She was only seventeen.

A thought struck her. Maybe her older brothers were more aware of what was going on back then? They might know something. Nathaniel was the oldest. He would have been away working by the time Melanie left. Ben was at university but lived at home on the farm on weekends. Geoff was too busy surfing to notice what anyone around him was doing, but she needed to ask him anyway.

Checking her watch, she decided to leave it until tomorrow. She needed something far more calming to occupy her time right now.

# Chapter 16

The main street was eerily quiet as Jenny pulled her Dodge ute up in front of Nikolic's Café. The café owner was known in town for fine coffee which made it her first stop every morning on the way to work.

The late autumn temperatures were colder than usual. At least Philips told her they were. She pulled a fleece zip-up jacket on over her uniform as she got out and stepped up to the front veranda.

The café wasn't the sort of place to sit outside and enjoy the view. Coober Pedy received less than eight inches of rainfall annually and this year, it came in one two-day rain event, back in March. The place turned to gloop that lasted the whole month, but now, like on any normal day, the dust rose with every passing car and floated onto the tables and chairs outside Niko's place.

Jenny nodded to the two grey-haired miners sitting outside in the dust. One sucked the life out of an almost spent rollie cigarette. The other puffed on a smouldering pipe.

'Hi guys.' She waved as she pulled the screen door open. Flies managed to find their way in, likely stuck to her back.

'Constable.' They nodded and spoke in unison as she let the door slam behind her.

'Hi Niko.' Jenny picked up the tray of coffees already waiting on the counter, including a cappuccino with two sugars for Philips who swore he'd never abandon his instant station coffee. In less than a month, he was a convert.

Scanning her card over the pay machine, she waved. 'Can't chat. Sorry.'

'Big case I hear.'

'Of course you heard. It's impossible to keep a lid on anything in this town.'

Niko grinned. 'Good luck.'

'Thanks.' She opened the screen door again, let it spring closed once more and hopped from the low concrete veranda.

As she opened the driver's side door, she noticed Tina Papadakis, sitting in a green hatchback, with a missing side mirror and lifting paintwork. Next to her was someone Jenny didn't recognise. No surprise there. Philips grew up here and knew everyone. She was still new in town so there was no way she was going to remember everyone anytime soon.

Realising Tina Papadakis' intimate life was none of her business, she slid into her car. Putting the coffees on the passenger seat, she started the engine and pulled out onto the main street. As she drove by, Tina and her friend slunk down in their seats as though they were hiding from her.

The hair on the back of her neck tingled. Why on earth were they hiding from anyone, especially from her?

********

An hour later, Jenny and Philips were on their way to interview the plasterer from Marj's office repair. The road out of town was dry and rough. The corrugations made the police Landcruiser skip and bounce.

'Overdue for a grader I reckon.' Philips' words vibrated as they left his lips.

'Nothing new about that.' Jenny braced herself with the side handle above the window. 'Where are we heading?' She recognised the road. There wasn't much out this way except station country.

'Con said the plasterer is onsite, working on refitting plasterboard to the teacher's accommodation at the Umoona Community.'

'I've been there once, with Nev. Met his Uncle, and some of the kids.' The memory of the sea of smiling faces made her stomach flutter. The Indigenous kids lead a different life. When she was growing up, kids went to school, sports, and in her case, worked on the farm. So many activities and responsibilities. The Community kids got to play, learn if they wanted to, then play some more.

She wondered how productive it was? If they left the community for the regular world, probably not very productive at all. At the same time, something in the back of her mind told her kids should be allowed to be kids for longer, no matter where they grow up.

'What brought you out here?'

Jenny considered telling Philips about her missing family members. With Sarge opening Nick's dad's murder investigation, it was bound to come out soon. But after last night's conversation with her dad, she didn't feel up to it. Not yet.

'Following up on something linked to a cold case. Sarge has the details.'

Philips glanced across at her, then snapped his eyes back on the road as the four-wheel drive hit a dip. They flew up into the air, before their seat belts locked up, dragging them back down and preventing their heads hitting the roof.

'Sorry about that.' Philips grinned sheepishly.

'All good.' She pressed her lips together to avoid smiling.

Philips steered the vehicle into the Community parking area, outside the gates. The excited, cheerful faces who greeted her last time looked on with wary curiosity as she stepped out of the Landcruiser.

Philips slammed the door and joined her as they entered through the open gates in the tall chainmail fence. Kids stepped out of the way like a wave as they entered. A group of women in colourful floral print dresses sat around a picnic table under the shelter where Jenny had once eaten hotdogs with Nev and his Uncle.

'Sorry to interrupt ladies,' she smiled. Blank faces stared back at her, until one of them recognised her.

'You're Nev's mate.'

'I am.' She tapped her uniform front. 'I'm working today, but nothing to do with anyone here.' She saw them all relax. 'Can you tell me where the workmen are today? We need to talk to one of them.'

'Only one fella here. In the schoolhouse.' The woman pointed down the single track leading into the Community. Jenny could see a large shed, a smaller brick building and more structures beyond.

She turned back, a frown on her forehead. The woman laughed. 'Can't miss him. He's the only other white fella here.' Her bright teeth shone against her dark skin.

'Thanks.' She and Philips wandered down the road, spotting a tradesman's four-wheel drive ute parked in front of an iron-clad house.

Philips knocked on the doorway, then stuck his head inside. 'Clive Watson,' he called. 'Can we have a word?'

The sound of a power tool continued uninterrupted. Philips snuck in, his eyes watchful in case he wandered into falling debris.

'Clive!' He yelled to the man standing on plastering stilts, his back to them, ear-pods in.

Clive spun around, teetering on the edge of losing balance. Philips rushed forward, arms extended for the catch, but years of skill and practice righted the tradie with little effort.

He pulled an earbud out, his loaded plaster trowel leaving a dob of finishing cement in his hair. His brow furrowed, bushy eyebrows knitted together.

'What can I do for you fine officers?' A broad grin split his lips.

'Just a few questions, about an old job you worked on.' Philips took the lead. Jenny let him. Tradies, especially out in the middle of nowhere often responded better to a guy than a girl. Stupid, but it was a reality not worth fighting over.

'Give me a sec to finish this mate.' He waved the loaded board and trowel. 'It will go off and be a bitch to clean up otherwise.' He noticed Jenny and blushed. 'Sorry luv.'

'No problem Clive. Nothing I haven't heard before.'

'Still. Anyway. If this goes off, I'll have a hell of a job cleaning my tools.'

'No worries. Carry on mate. Don't mind if we watch?' Philips encouraged him to turn back to his work.

'Nah mate.'

'Always wondered how the hell anyone balanced on those things.'

'Easy once you get the hang of it.' Clive slapped finishing plaster on, wiped it off with the edge of his trowel and repeated with unexpected speed and agility until the load on his flat board was gone.

'Looks sweet.' Philips admired the job. 'What did you need to fix?'

Clive chuckled as he untied his stilts, stepped out and indicated he was taking his tools out to clean. 'Some kids welcomed the new teacher, back in February when school term started. Didn't realise they'd caused a leak until the heavy downpour in March.'

Clive wandered to an outside water tank, turned on the tap and started to rinse his tools into a bucket. 'Hold your nose guys. The water out here is a bit on the nose.'

A pungent odour stung Jenny's eyes. 'What the hell is that?'

'Sulphur luv. The water pumped out of the ground out here is full of it.'

'That's awful.' She stepped back, trying not to hold her nose.

He carried on cleaning without a fuss. 'You get used to it. What job did you need info on?'

With the lightning speed of the bush telegraph, Jenny expected him to know. Maybe he'd been out here all week.

'The Opal Inn Motel reception, about five years back.'

He nodded, shook his trowel off and placed it on the board. 'Yep. I remember that one. Why?'

Philips gave her a sideways glance. The tradesman hadn't flinched. He didn't know about the body being found, but more importantly, he didn't look even remotely worried someone might find something.

'An old lady rammed her car through the front on Saturday.' Still no reaction except an expected purse of the lips and nod. 'We found a body in the debris.' That got a response, but only a raised eyebrow.

'Damn.'

'It was inside the wall, wrapped in plastic.' He was still nodding as though someone were telling him the weather report. 'Under the plasterboard.' Still nodding, until he wasn't.

'Hey wait up a minute. You don't think.' He put his hands up defensively. 'I remember that job. I didn't plaster it all. I thought it was weird. Con only uses me and my team, but the board was fitted fine, so I didn't think anything of it.'

'What do you mean?'

'I got back to the job, I don't know, on the Thursday, or maybe the Friday. Two sheets were up. Thought it was weird, but it was a professional enough looking job. I left it, fitted the rest of the boards, then flushed it.'

'And you're not sure if it was Thursday or Friday of that week?' Jenny pushed for more details. A timeline could certainly make their job easier.

Clive rubbed his chin. 'Had to be a Thursday. I finished the job, final skim coat Saturday morning. Trying real hard to get Marj's office back up and going before the Rally crew came in on the Sunday. It wasn't painted, but it was sealed up ready.'

Coober Pedy was on the route of multiple charity rally races. Jenny made a mental note to check with Marj on the dates to confirm Clive's story, but if he was telling the truth – and he behaved like he was, then at least a timeline could be established, placing Franny's body inside the wall on the Wednesday night.

Now they needed to find out who saw her in the days leading up to her death. Philips thanked Clive. They turned to leave, but Jenny stopped.

'Why did welcoming the teacher in February make a hole for rain to get in?'

Clive laughed. 'The kids threw some rocks on the roof, to scare the new teacher. One was a bit bigger than the rest. Knocked the top off a screw.'

'Rocks?' Jenny was stunned, but Philips nearly choked on a laugh.

'Yep. Apparently it's quite the initiation out here. Most of the teachers are fresh out of teacher's college. Trying to do the remote work to clock up brownie points so they can secure a cushy spot with the Education Department. Remote service gives them priority job choice, but most only last three months.'

'Really!'

'The kids don't mean any harm. They just don't live by the same rules out here.'

'I'm glad I became a cop not a teacher then.' Jenny waved. 'Thanks for the help.'

'Anytime.'

# Chapter 17

It was after lunch when they arrived back at the station. A quick stop at the bakery and they were sitting in front of the murder board on display in Sarge's office, away from public view. A photo of Marj and the victim occupied a lot of white space.

Jenny bit into her chicken pie. Philips did the same, hand cupped below his chin, trying not to drop crumbs of filo pastry all over the boss's floor.

'We'll need to check with the carpenter. See where the job was at when he finished up.' Jenny recapped their interview with the plasterer.

O'Connell flicked through a couple of printed sheets. 'Tom Hammond was the carpenter on the job, but we don't have contact information on him in Con's files.'

'I'll phone Con.' Philips spoke from the doorway, his mouth half full, breathing over his hot pie before chewing it.

'I'll run him through the registration office, see if he has a car registered in his name and a current licence with address details.' Jenny turned to leave.

'Actually, you two need to hear this.' Sarge formed a steeple with his fingers in his lap as he reclined into the office chair.

Philips turned back. Jenny stopped.

'We now have *three* cold cases. They all need equal attention, so we need to divide and conquer.'

'Three?' Philips frowned. O'Connell waited. He knew what was coming.

Sarge waved at Jenny to tell the story. She prepared herself, expecting Philips to be annoyed she didn't tell him early. Wondering where to start, she delayed by adjusting her ponytail, carefully studying his puzzled features as they focussed on her.

'You know about Nick's dad, Ron?' Philips nodded. 'That case is officially reopened, but it seems it might be connected to a cold case from my hometown.'

'Get on with it Williams.' Sarge coaxed with his usual lack of tact.

'Sorry Sir.' She turned her gaze back to Philips. 'I'm sorry I didn't mention it earlier. Long story short, I came here to track down my cousin and aunt. They went missing while holidaying in the area.' Philip's eyes widened. 'It appears they may still be alive and well and part of a runaway relocation program Ron and Patricia Johnston were operating.'

It took Philips a moment to absorb the information. His reaction was not what she was expecting.

'That's good news, isn't it? Them probably being alive and all?' Philips' expression was genuinely concerned. The guy had a big heart and always believed the best in people. It was both a blessing and a curse in police work.

'I hope so. Nick and I found a ledger at the farm, in the cellar, full of coded entries. We believe they are related to the runaways.' She couldn't bring herself to believe Melanie and Aunt Carolyn were linked to domestic violence, so she didn't mention it. But she realised she never ran a background check on them or Uncle Pete.

'Someone in that book might have relatives desperate enough to find them to kill Ron and kidnap Patricia.' O'Connell carried on the story.

'We need someone who isn't too close to this to dig deeper.' Sarge gave her an apologetic look. 'Philips. Run background on Melanie and Carolyn Williams. Williams will give you the details.' He nodded in her direction. She opened her mouth to protest. 'You'd be the first person to tell any of us we are too close and we need to keep this investigation neat and tidy in case something goes astray.'

Jenny sighed. He was right. She didn't like it one little bit though. 'Can I still be in the loop? And help with working out the code in the book? I think I can be of help there. I'll see any link to my cousin.'

Sarge and O'Connell exchanged a look. Understanding passed between them. 'Under supervision.'

Jenny saluted. 'Thanks Sarge. I'll phone Con and run the registration and licence details for Hammond.'

'Good. Philips. You follow up on those background checks. I'm going to see if I can work this ledger out for now.' O'Connell lifted the book from Sarge's desk and followed them out of his office.

Philips crossed the office toward the front counter computer. Jenny headed to the computer on O'Connell's workstation. O'Connell searched for another spot to sit and check over the coded ledger.

'We need another workstation.' He puffed out his cheeks as he strode past the desk. 'I'll be in the lunchroom. Call me if you need me.'

'Will do Sir.' Jenny pulled the chair out, sat and considered looking up Tom Hammond on the registration office but decided Con was the easiest place to start. He employed Hammond, so would likely have an address where they could start looking for him. Dialling *Papa Construction* using the desk phone, she waited while it rang a few times.

'*Papa Construction*, Tina speaking.' The voice was timid, but clear and polite.

'Tina. It's Constable Williams, we met the other day.'

'Yes.' Her answer was tentative.

'I need some contact information on one of your contractors. He worked on Marj's office, back in two-thousand and ten.'

'Oh.'

'Do I need to speak with your dad?'

'No. Which contractor?'

'Tom Hammond.' Silence. 'Are you there Tina?'

'Sorry. Yes. Um Tom doesn't work for us anymore.'

'Do you have a current address for him?'

'No.' The answer came quickly.

'O..kay. Can I speak with Con or your mum? Maybe they know someone who knows him.'

'Tom finished working for us years ago.'

There was something in the tone of her voice telling Jenny it wasn't on good terms. He was likely in the system with a driver's licence or car registration details so she decided now wasn't the time to force the issue, but her gut knotted. Did Tom leaving have anything to do with the dead woman in Marj's office wall?

'Okay. Thanks for your time Tina. I'll find him another way.'

For a second, Jenny thought she might be ready to say something. 'Bye.' The phone went dead. Whatever it was, Tina Papadakis thought better of it.

# Chapter 18

The computer cursor blinked as the registration office churned over Tom Hammond's details. 'Got an address.' Philips turned around. 'It's just north of town.' She glanced at her watch. 'If he's working, he should be finishing up soon.'

'Yeah, but he could be in a pub or anywhere but home.'

'We'll call by. Leave a calling card. I'll run a phone search while we wait for him to get back to us. Maybe we can find a mobile number registered in his name.'

'Okay. Let's go.' Philips met her at the bank of lockers alongside the desk she was working at.

Jenny always got an energy hit when she could get away from the office work to interview people, drive around town, or catch up with the locals. It was one of the reasons she enjoyed police work.

Retrieving her utility vest, she checked her taser, locked the locker and signed out her service weapon.

'I'll let O'Connell know we are heading out.' Philips disappeared down the hallway, returning a moment later with the Senior Constable who made a beeline for his favourite chair behind the only desk in the small office area.

Jenny wondered where they were going to fit another workstation, and why they needed one now and not before, but her mind drifted back to Philips and the checks he was running earlier.

'Did you find anything on my family?' She waited by the counter for Philips to collect the police Landcruiser keys.

'Nothing. No criminal records on your aunt, cousin or uncle. No domestic disturbances. No child services reports. There was one mandated report from a youth group pastor.'

Philips pressed the *unlock* on the key fob as they approached the vehicle. Jenny's hand rested on the door handle of the passenger's side.

'Mandated report, from a pastor? We never went to church.'

'Youth group pastors do all sorts of stuff. They are sometimes part of the Chaplaincy program in public schools.' Philips opened his door and slid in behind the wheel. 'I'll check with the school guidance counsellor's records when we get back.'

'Okay. Thanks.' Jenny fastened her seatbelt, her mind running memories of her school years with Melanie.

'It's probably nothing.' Philips reassured her as he started the car, his hand hovering over the shift, but not engaging the gears. His gaze fell on hers, his expression confused. 'Why didn't you tell me?' He wasn't annoyed, only hurt shone in his eyes.

'I wanted to. Honestly. I just wasn't sure how I was going to approach the whole investigation. Sarge and I didn't exactly get along to begin with. I was afraid he'd sack me and send me home if he knew.'

'I would have kept your secret.' Philips shoved the car into gear and drove off. 'Where are we heading?' His quick change of subject was welcomed.

'Out on Seventeen Mile Road.' Philips nodded.

Jenny wanted to explain more to Philips but was unsure what to say. She probably should have trusted him, but she didn't know when she arrived, how nice a guy he was. The day he greeted her at the airport, he was friendly enough. When they started working together, she mistook his chivalry for chauvinism, and it was Penny who gave her a pep talk about making assumptions.

The Landcruiser turned left and headed north of town toward the Breakaway National Park. The eroded mountain ridge came into view. A tinge of green peppered the hill, left over from the heavy rain in March.

The area was full of culturally significant sites and was a scientist's haven, with fossils dating back millions of years – when the sea covered inland Australia. It was bizarre to think this dry, desolate piece of red earth was once at the bottom of the ocean.

'Corner of Koska Street.' Jenny clarified as Philips slowed down along the narrow bitumen road. 'That's it.' Jenny pointed to a dirty red brick home. The olive-coloured iron roof dated the construction to the eighties, but nothing else about the drab architecture told a story.

Philips drove the Landcruiser up into the driveway. The single carport housed a green sedan, jogging Jenny's memory.

'I saw Tina Papadakis with a guy in that car.' She nodded to the rear end of the vehicle. One taillight was cracked, but functioning. The hatchback boot was tied down with a thick, black cable tie.

'So Tina knows the guy. Nothing unusual there. He worked for her dad.'

'True, but they went to a lot of effort not to be seen in the vehicle when I drove by.' Philips lifted an eyebrow, undid his seatbelt and got out. They simultaneously adjusted their waist belts and checked the clip was over their weapon before approaching the house.

Jenny pressed the doorbell, but nothing sounded inside and no light blinked to indicate it was working. She waited a few seconds, heard nothing, then knocked on the door.

She glanced around the yard while she waited. There were no plants in the garden. The gravel driveway was the only thing breaking up the dirt surrounding the building. An old couch with torn fabric and a crate of empty beer bottles alongside sat under the veranda.

'The car's here,' she noted, then knocked again.

They listened, no television or radio noise filtered through the door, but Jenny heard an internal door slam, glanced at Philips who nodded he heard it too. Stepping back, they gave themselves space.

'I'm coming!' The door opened to reveal a tall, lean man with a dark blonde scraggly long beard and tiny eyes lost below bristly eyebrows. 'Ah.' He glanced from Philips to Jenny and back. 'What's up?'

'Are you Tom Hammond?' Philips stepped forward, obviously wanting to take the lead. Jenny let him. The guy appeared rough and Philips always struggled to keep his chivalry in check despite their agreement that she could hold her own.

The man gazed nervously over their shoulders. Maybe he was checking for back up? Was he expecting them or some other sort of trouble? Jenny wondered what he might want to hide, other than being seen in public with Tina Papadakis.

'Yes.' He finally made eye contact with Philips. 'Why?'

'You used to work for Con Papadakis?' Philips continued. Tom nodded. 'Did you work on a job at the *Opal Inn Motel* back in two thousand and ten, fixing the reception area after a vehicle impact?'

'Yeah. It was my last job with Con.'

'Are you working with anyone now?' Jenny interrupted.

'I wish.' He rubbed his chin, maybe contemplating if he should share more. 'Con bloody runs the construction industry in this town. If you don't work for him, you don't work for anyone.'

She glanced into the front entrance of the home. Tom pulled the door closed behind his back. She carried on with another question.

'That must be tough. Why did you stop working for him? Did you two have a falling out?'

Tom shrugged. 'It's ancient history.' He huffed and crossed his arms over his chest. A sure sign he wasn't elaborating.

Jenny couldn't help wondering if the disagreement might be related to their case, but now wasn't the time to get heavy handed. They needed him talking, freely.

'Did you see anything suspicious about the job?' Philips took over the questioning.

'No.' He tightened his arms defensively. 'Why?'

'Just routine questions Mr Hammond.' Philips sounded very formal. Jenny was impressed. 'At what stage did you finish up on the job?'

'Studs were done. External cladding was fixed. It was all set for plasterboard.'

'Did you leave your tools on site the Wednesday night?'

Tom rubbed his beard, ran his fingers through it, catching a sticky spot. Jenny fought to keep her stomach in check.

'Come to think of it, I might have. Con sacked me. I was pretty pissed off, so I went to the underground bar for beers with a few mates. I didn't get back there until Thursday mid-morning.'

It sounded plausible. Someone used a nail gun to hold Franny's body in place while they plastered over her. Was Tom making the story up to cover his butt?

'Can you name the guys you drank with? We'd like to confirm.' Philips jotted details down in his notepad.

'Why? What's this about?'

'Mr Hammond. A body was recovered from inside the wall of the motel office after a recent crash. You didn't know?' His eyes grew wide.

'Shit!' He rubbed his beard vigorously. 'No bloody way. I can see where this is going, but I didn't plaster the place. I'm a chippy.'

'We know that Mr Hammond, but nail gun nails were found in the victim.' Philips and Jenny watched as Tom turned a pale shade of green.

'Oh that's foul. You think my nail gun…' He gagged.

'Can we grab those names Mr Hammond?' He nodded, pulled out his mobile phone and started retrieving details.

# Chapter 19

Philips reversed out the driveway, pulled back on to Seventeen Mile Road and drove back into town. 'What do you think?'

'I think he was pretty surprised to find out about the body and either he's a good actor, or there is no way he could have nailed Franny's body to the studs without puking his guts up.'

'Something for Penny to check for, on the victim maybe?'

'Maybe, but I don't like him for it.'

Philips sighed. 'Nah, me neither. I thought you might ask him about Tina though.'

'Thought about it, but at this stage I don't think it's relevant.'

'Where to next then?'

'Let's call back in on Con Papadakis again. I'd like to know why he sacked Tom, on the day Franny died. Someone, with intimate knowledge of working with plasterboard and nail guns, killed Franny and hid her body in the wall.'

'And you think it could be Con? What's his motive?'

'Let's ask him and find out.' Jenny grinned.

Philips nodded, turned left and drove towards Con's yard.

Five minutes later, they pulled up outside the metal-clad offices. Jenny stepped out of the vehicle to the sound of raised voices, just like last time. It seemed all was not peaceful in the Papadakis household.

Jenny slammed the car door, but not before nodding toward the noise to make sure Philips could hear. The voices stopped as the door thudded shut. Tina Papadakis scurried from the office toward the ladies' toilets. Her head down, her feet moving rapidly over the metal ramp.

Jenny adjusted her hip belt and led the way up to the main office. Con appeared flushed, even with his olive skin. Like last time, Mrs Papadakis sat at the back, behind a desk, except Jenny could see her chest heaving.

Philips begged her with his eyes to take the lead. It puzzled her, because only a few months ago, she watched him calmly get an old lady to lower her shot gun from his face on their first major case together, but it seemed a domestic was outside his realm of expertise.

Jenny grew up in a family business. Dairy farming, with the family, was always tough. Heated rows were common. But this looked like something a little more than cash flow discussions or when the hay should be cut.

'Mr Papadakis. Sorry to bother you again.' She wasn't sorry at all, but the man was staring at her with distaste. Her stomach rolled. What was his issue? Female cops maybe?

'What do you want?' Jenny ignored his rudeness. It wasn't worth arguing over, unless it escalated.

'Sir. You employed a carpenter, Tom Hammond.' His brow creased, and his eyes squinted in a way that made Jenny's arms break out in goose bumps.

'That useless Yamimeno Vlaka.' Jenny didn't need to understand the language. Con's posture said it all. Maybe this was why Tina didn't want to be seen with Tom or let her talk to Con about him?

'I can see you didn't appreciate him Mr Papadakis. Was it his workmanship you didn't care for?' She was certain it was nothing to do with Tom's skill. Con huffed, puffed, snorted through his nostrils but failed to find any words at first.

'Nothing to do with your case.' He waved his hand dismissively.

'How about you let us be the judge of that.' She glanced at Philips, his note pad was out, his pencil scribbling furiously.

Con watched him with eagle eyes, then licked his lips as though assessing what he could keep to himself.

'Tom dated Tina. They were friends in school. Con didn't like the boy.' Jenny watched Mrs Papadakis rise slowly from her solitude way back in the corner of the office. Con sneered at her. He didn't want her talking about their private life.

'And you didn't like him either?' Jenny addressed Mrs Papadakis with the question.

'I did. Con didn't.' She glanced at her husband as she spoke. Her tone unusually calm in contrast to Con's.

Jenny turned back to Con. 'He was good enough to work for you. Why not good enough to date your daughter?'

Con bounced his thumbs together, holding his fingers in a tight grip with one another. He was wired, angry, ready to explode, but still able to carefully judge what needed to be shared with her.

'Unless you want to arrest me Constable, I suggest you leave. I don't need to discuss my business practices or my family matters with you. If you come up with formal charges, let my lawyer know.' He stormed around the counter, yanked a drawer open with enough force to dislodge it, and pulled out a card which he thrust in Jenny's face.

The interview was over. Jenny glanced at Mrs Papadakis as she sulked back to her desk, hidden in the hollows at the rear of the office. She needed to get the woman alone. But how?

# Chapter 20

The whiteboard was filling up fast. Jenny picked up the black marker pen and started writing up details.

'So Tom Hammond said he left his tools on site because Con sacked him when he finished on Wednesday.' She wrote the details on the board next to the plasterer's details. 'Plasterer said two panels of plasterboard were up already when he got there to start the job on Thursday at seven a.m., so we have a timeline.'

'Who had access to the site Wednesday night then?' O'Connell waited by the door, one eye on the front desk.

'Con would have. I think he knows something.' She spoke with her back to the room. Philips sat on the edge of Sarge's desk scoffing a hotdog.

'What makes you say that?' Sarge sat forward and leant on his desk.

'He sacked Tom, the same day Franny was killed.' Jenny glanced back as she answered, then returned her focus to making notes on the whiteboard.

'That doesn't mean he knows anything about the murder. He might just not like the guy.'

'That was obvious.' Jenny summarised their interview. 'Mrs Papadakis said it had something to do with Tina and Tom dating in school, but there was something more to it.'

'We don't have any motive for Con to kill Franny, and why would he dump her body in the office wall? Why not remove it and take it somewhere else? He's not tall, but he's a well-built guy. He could have dropped the victim down a mine or something?' O'Connell stepped away from the doorway as Philips finished eating.

Philips tossed his rubbish in the bin next to Sarge's desk and returned to his usual spot, leaning against the door frame and keeping watch on the front counter. The station in Coober Pedy was small. The officers all did day shift, and night shift if required. It was rare, because most days were over by three, especially in summer.

'Good point.' Philips agreed. 'Con is what, over a hundred kilos and it isn't all fat. He could have dragged the body out easily after dark and dumped it.'

'Maybe he was interrupted, by Marj or one of the bar staff leaving late?' Jenny added Con's name to the board, circled it and put a question mark next to it with the word MOTIVE. Then ALIBI.

'We are missing something.' Sarge pressed his laptop closed and reached for his car keys. 'But we're not going to find it right now.' He strode toward the door. 'We'll pick this up tomorrow.'

Jenny watched his retreating back and turned her questioning gaze on O'Connell. 'Do we add details about the other cases here too?'

O'Connell stepped toward her, pulled the whiteboard away from the wall and spun it around to reveal another crime board. This one featured a photo of Nick's dad's crime scene right in the middle.

'Update it now, turn it back around and I'll see you both tomorrow.' He strolled toward the doorway, stopped and turned back. 'Don't stay on it, just add the details and go catch up with McGregor. I think she heads back tomorrow.'

Jenny didn't need any encouragement. She jotted down her cousin and aunt's details from memory. They were ingrained in her memory after years of worrying about what happened to them. Could they be alive? Was it too much to hope for?

Philips stepped up, added the details about the mandated report from the pastor. 'I'll follow this up tomorrow. Promise.'

'Thanks Philips. I'm kinda glad you're on this with me now.'

'Me too. If they ran away, there is a really good chance they are still hiding.'

*Yes, but from who or what?* She didn't say the words aloud. To do that, would mean she must have missed something important all those years ago. She thought about her dad's reaction and her stomach knotted.

Her whole purpose for becoming a cop was to find Melanie. Now she was getting closer, she was afraid she didn't want to discover the truth of what happened all those years ago.

'See you tomorrow. You right to lock up?'

'Sure.' Philips waved her out of the office. 'Say bye to Penny for me?'

'Will do.' Jenny rushed to her locker, grabbed her backpack, stowed her utility vest and packed her weapon away in the gun safe.

Two minutes later she abandoned her bag in her car and jogged toward the Motel, slowing as she reached the reception area. Her mind churned over scenarios for why Con would stow the body in the wall.

Scanning the area, she noted it wasn't well lit. No streetlights, two exits from reception , one leading to the carpark only steps away. He could have easily wrapped her body in the same builders' plastic they found it in and put it in his work truck. No one would have been the wiser.

Without a motive, all they could do was trace the victim's last days and see if anyone bore a grudge against her, other than Marj.

She pushed the glass door open and stepped into the expansive front bar and restaurant. Worn commercial carpet was covered by locals milling around. Stan waved from behind the glossy wooden bar. Penny sat a few stools away from him, chatting with Tim and Nev.

The sound of muffled conversation enveloped her in familiarity. The tension in her neck and shoulders eased as she approached her friends.

The new girl Kelly greeted her. 'Beer?'

'Yes thanks.' Kelly got to work, ignoring the noise and conversation around her. 'Where are you from Kelly? I'm not local myself, so I know it can be hard to connect here.'

The woman peered up, the corners of her mouth twitched, but not in a happy way. 'I'm here for a fresh start, so let's leave it at that.'

'Noted.' Jenny was aware she was still in uniform. Was Kelly's background illegal? She shoved the thought aside. The woman was making a fresh start. She deserved a chance. 'Coober Pedy is full of people just like you. Welcome, even if I'm not local enough to officially welcome anyone.'

Kelly handed the beer over. Jenny held her gaze. 'Eight bucks thanks.'

Pulling out her credit card, ready to scan it over the machine and pay, she stopped a moment. 'If you ever need someone to talk to, I'm here, without the badge.' The woman passed the eftpos machine up. Jenny scanned her card. Kelly nodded, her expression unreadable.

'See you around.' Jenny didn't know what else to say. Coober Pedy was remote. People came out here for all sorts of reasons. To get rich, which was rarer than most expected. To live cheap on unemployment benefits. To run away from their past, like Melanie and Aunt Carolyn might have. Maybe that was what Kelly was doing? The thought made her wonder if

Kelly's details were in the ledger from the William Creek Homestead?

'Hey.' Penny turned from her conversation. 'Let's grab a seat. I'm starving and it's my last night.'

'Yeah. O'Connell said you were done.' The boys picked up their beers and the group made their way through the dining room to a round table by the front window.

'Everything is packed up and on the way to the lab.'

'Nothing more interesting popped up I assume, or you would have told me. Right?'

Penny put a cardboard coaster under her wine glass. 'I found a piece of jewellery, probably Marj's. I've photographed it and sent it with the evidence heading back to Adelaide.'

'Do you have the photo here?'

'No! It's drinks time, not work time.' She lifted her wineglass up in front of Jenny, then made a show of sipping it to emphasize her point.

Jenny put her hands up in surrender. 'Okay. Okay. You're right.' She spotted Marj coming out of the kitchen. 'I just need to ask Marj something.'

'But I want to order fooood.'

'Me too.' Nev pulled the chair out next to her and sat heavily, Tim did the same on the opposite side of the table next to Penny.

'Wish you didn't have to go back to the big smoke tomorrow.' Tim watched Penny shuffle the menus out to everyone.

Jenny fought with herself between being rude to her friends and her need to speak with Marj. The latter won out, despite the look Tim was giving Penny and the niggling sensation in the back of Jenny's mind that she might have been too busy to notice something more serious developing between her friends.

'Order me a schnitzel. I'll pay you back.' She hopped up from her seat as Nev opened his mouth to speak. Then shut it quickly.

'In wine?' Penny seemed unaware of Tim's lingering gaze or the statement he made a moment ago.

'You got it.' Jenny turned to Nev. 'Sorry. I'll be back in a sec. This case has me running around like a loon. I've got news about my cousin's case too.'

As she shuffled away between their table and the next, she heard Nev groan over leaving him hanging. The smell of body odour brought tears to her eyes as she squeezed past two men covered in opal mine dust to meet Marj at the edge of the bar.

'Evening Jenny.' Marj's hair was a new, brighter, more orange shade of red today. Her smile broad and cheerful despite the broken arm in a cast.

'Hi Marj.' She bit her lip wondering how to ask about the Motel owner's conversation with Tina. She knew it was none of her business, but her instincts were seeing connections that didn't make sense. Tina's outburst, the stealthy rendezvous with Tom Hammond, Con's behaviour today. If they hadn't just pulled a murder victim out of the motel wall where all these people were connected, she wouldn't have thought much of it, but they had.

'What do you need luv?' Marj tapped her arm gently. 'Spit it out.'

'You were talking with Tina yesterday and she got upset. I was just wondering...'

'What it was about?'

Jenny nodded. 'Yes. I know it's none of my business, but I thought it might be related to our investigation.'

'Tina was Jason's goddaughter and I've known her since she was a baby. She used to come around a lot, until Jason died. She's just having a tough time right now.'

'I saw her with Tom Hammond the other day. She seemed to be trying extremely hard not to be spotted with him.' Jenny knew she was pushing her friendship with Marj, asking for personal details about Tina, but the dynamics in the Papadakis family seemed off.

'It's a long story, but Tina is promised to a friend of the Papadakis family.'

'Promised! What year are we living in?' Jenny realised her voice rose a pitch, and glanced around to make sure no one overheard.

'Traditions run deep for Con.'

'I can see why she is keeping her relationship with Tom quiet then. Poor woman.'

# Chapter 21

The dugout was oppressively quiet as Jenny tossed her keys on the kitchen bench. Tim and Nev were on late shift, which started right after they left the restaurant.

She rounded the kitchen bench, reached for a glass from the wooden shelf and ran herself a drink of water. Half emptying the contents in a long gulp, she put it down and rested her hands on the sink.

Thinking of the phone call with her dad the previous night brought a lump to her throat. Her soul ached, but she didn't know what to do about it. Her phone buzzed in her pocket. Reception was horrible in the unit, but text messages often snuck through.

Glancing at the screen, her whole body relaxed. *Call me when you can.* Nick's timing was perfect. She finished her water and dialled his number as she left the dugout.

The stars were a spectacular blanket in a clear sky. The phone rang twice.

'Hey.' She spoke as soon as the line connected.

'Hey yourself. I'm not interrupting?'

'No. Just got home. I was going to call you anyway.' She sat down on a weathered log in the drought-proof garden of white gravel and succulents. Her voice echoed into the night, silencing the crickets nearby.

'What about?'

'You go first. You texted me.'

'I just wanted to hear your voice.'

Jenny smiled, butterflies burst to life in her stomach. 'I wanted to talk to you too. It's been a long few days. I wish you lived close by.' *I need a hug!*

'So do I.'

The tone of his voice curled her toes, making her realise she might need more than a hug, but the distance between them wasn't ideal.

Nick had responsibilities. Running the property occupied a lot of his time and as much as she wanted to be there to help him, she wanted to solve both family mysteries too. They were making the commute. They could keep making it work.

'I did have something I wanted to off load on you. If you don't mind?'

'Anytime.' She heard a chair scrape on the floor. Nick was living in the workmen's quarters while out at the station during the week. Someone had to oversee the property and until the homestead was rebuilt, he was stuck sharing space with his staff.

'I called my mum last night. Wanted to speak with her, because speaking to my dad is always hard, but anyway, she put dad on.' She was rambling already. Stopping, she sucked in a breath and blew it out with her cheeks. How was she going to explain this to Nick?

'You okay?'

'Yeah. Sorry.' Burning behind her eyes signalled another bout of tears were at the ready.

'Don't be.' The sound of laughter in the background told her he wasn't alone. 'Give me a sec.' A door opened, then slammed. 'That's better.'

'I told dad we found out Melanie and Aunt Carolyn might be alive. That they might have run away.' She swallowed hard. 'He got angry Nick. I don't understand.' Hot tears broke free, rolling down her cheeks.

There was a moment of silence as Nick considered his answer. 'Think of it from your dad's perspective. If your aunt

98

ran away with her daughter, she either abandoned his brother, or there was a reason she took off.'

'I don't want to believe Uncle Pete did anything to make them leave, but…'

'But if Mrs B. is right, mum and dad only helped people in trouble.'

'Right.' She wiped her face with the back of her hand and covered the phone mic as she sniffed.

'Don't be too hard on your dad. Your relationship with your family is important.' Jenny swallowed back more tears. Feeling sorry for herself was pitiful when she thought about Nick's family. His parents were gone, one dead, one missing. He was right. Her family was alive, and she needed to be thankful for them – even if her dad was pig-headed at times.

'You're right.' She thought about Nev's *Sorry Business* and the diary she and Nick found in the Homestead cellar before the fire. 'Did you ever read your grandmother's diary?'

'No. Why?'

'Nick, you might still have family you don't know about.' She agonised over telling him or not, but it was plain to see if he read the diary and one day he might, then he'd be annoyed she didn't mention it.

'What do you mean?'

'I read your grandmother's diary. It's quite informative. I don't want to jump to conclusions, but you might be related to the locals, closer than you think.'

He chuckled. 'Sounds like I better read it then. Do you still have it?'

'I do. I'll give it to you this weekend.'

'You don't want to give me a hint?'

'I think you should read it for yourself.'

'Sounds like a plan. Any luck with the ledger?'

'No. Sarge has it right now and this current case has us a bit tied up, but I'm hoping to spend some time going over it tomorrow. Do you have any idea what code your mum and dad might have used?'

'None. Mum was a crossword fiend, but dad avoided paperwork like the plague.'

'I'd give anything to decipher it. Someone in that book could easily be the reason your dad was murdered.'

The sound of laughter drifted in the background. 'Sorry. The guys are playing cards. Can your tech people have a go at the ledger?'

'You should join them.'

'Maybe later.' He didn't sound convinced of the idea.

'I'll pass it on to the techs if we can't crack it this week. They won't prioritise anything on a cold case.'

'I've waited this long, I can wait a bit longer.'

# Chapter 22

Phillips was already standing in front of the front desk computer as Jenny wandered into the office, her backpack over one shoulder, a tray of coffees in her left hand.

'Coffee's up.' She lifted the countertop, ducked under and closed it carefully.

Philips didn't look up, his eyes were fixed on the screen. Jenny frowned, stopped next to him, scanned over his shoulder at what he was focussed on and put his coffee on the counter next to him.

'What's up?'

'Oh!' He jumped. She grinned. 'I emailed the Pastor we talked about. He doesn't recall anything specifically, but I requested a copy of the mandated report he lodged. I was going over it now.'

'Oh.' She wondered if she wanted to see what it contained or not. 'Let me know once you have. I'll check it out.' She crossed the room to O'Connell's desk, put his coffee down and glanced around to see if Sarge was in yet.

His door was ajar. Taking his coffee, she approached, stopped, listened, then knocked. 'Sarge?'

'Come in Williams.'

She pushed the door open, strode to his desk and put his coffee down. 'Can I grab the ledger and take a look Sir?'

'Have you got an idea?'

'I did a bit of Googling last night for common ciphers. I want to try a few out and see if it might be a match.'

Sarge pursed his lips, nodded, then opened the top drawer of his desk. The ledger thudded as he dropped it onto his desk. 'Give it a go, but make sure you keep up with the

Franny Kovac case. I've had the local paper chasing me for an update.'

'They could be helpful Sir. Maybe we could ask them to run a story, asking about anyone who saw the victim in the lead up to her death? Especially on the Wednesday night.'

'You know I don't like to stir up the locals Williams. If we start asking for help, they'll think we don't have it in hand and then Marj will be off on a tangent, claiming we have a serial killer in town, like that arson case.'

'Actually. Marj has been awfully quiet about this Sarge. I know Franny was family, but still. Usually she goes all *Murder She Wrote* on me and starts theorising.'

Sarge sat back, rubbed his chin and nodded. 'You're right. You better check on her today. Maybe she's taken this harder than we thought. Franny was Jason's sister and she *was* hidden in *her* office wall for nearly five years.'

'I'll grab lunch at the motel. I need to identify a piece of jewellery found in the debris in any case. Penny is sending photos once she gets to the lab this morning.'

'Put it on the board once you get it.'

'I will Sir, but it wasn't found where the body was uncovered, so Penny believes it might not be related.'

'That car hit at sixty k's. Crap will have flown everywhere.'

'I'm sure she's keeping that in mind Sir.'

Sarge picked up his coffee. 'Thanks.'

'No worries.' Jenny turned and left the office.

Philips spoke as she returned. 'Got it here.'

Jenny stopped, her legs grew suddenly heavy. Could this one mandatory report be why she ran away? But why would Aunt Carolyn go too?

Philips held up one single piece of paper. She closed the space between as though she were walking on the moon.

Her hand automatically plucked the paper from his fingers. Her eyes scanned the words but her mind felt foggy, detached.

The report contained the pastor's name and Philips was right, he was acting as the school chaplain. Jenny racked her brain to picture him, but she couldn't. She didn't even recall why Melanie would have seen him. They weren't a church going family. The girls had never been to Sunday school or youth group.

Was this guy grooming her? Did this guy chase Melanie out of Victor Harbor?

She scanned the rest of the report. A teacher had asked the chaplain to build a rapport with Melanie, in an informal setting, to gauge her behaviour. Jenny thought back. Melanie was a straight A student. Popular, pretty, smart, and always in good favour with the teachers.

*Melanie is defensive when asked about her family. I noted bruising around her elbow and upper arm and when I moved toward her, she flinched. I'm making this mandatory report in case there are other cases that might warrant a further investigation into this young woman's family life or other relationships that may be impacting on her life.*

Bruises. Reflexive behaviour. As a grown woman and a police officer, Jenny had undergone mandatory reporting training. As a chaplain or counsellor, this man would have been obliged to record his concerns with Child Safety. They wouldn't act unless multiple reports were lodged.

This was standard practice because one nosey neighbour reporting child abuse shouldn't warrant removing the children into care, but multiple complaints, from many sources could.

Was this why no one wanted her to search for her cousin? Did her parents *know* something was up? A knot formed in her stomach and a lump in her throat made swallowing difficult.

Jenny drew a deep, focussed breath. 'Can I show this to Sarge?'

'Sure.' Philips watched Jenny retreat to the back office. 'Sir?'

'Come in Williams.' Gruff as always.

Jenny drifted into Sarge's office, her mind telling her this couldn't be happening. 'I just read the school chaplain's report on Melanie Sir and I'm wondering…'

'Spit it out.'

'I know you don't like to draw attention to crime in town and I know you wanted to keep the investigation into Ron Johnston's murder under wraps for now, but…'

Sarge pointed to his 'hot seat', the place where she endured many lectures on her first few weeks in town. She sat. He leant forward. 'What do you want Williams?'

She wanted to put a spin on her request. One that would make it sound as though it were in the Police's best interests, but she couldn't find one.

'I'd like to put a BOLO out on Melanie's description. I'd like to run a licence and passport facial recognition to find her, but if that fails Sir, I'd like to give a press release. Melanie and Aunt Carolyn were one of a handful of runaways who were at William Creek Station just before Ron Johnston was murdered. I think these cases could be connected.'

Her running sentence left her breathless, the heat rushed to her cheeks.

'I can't issue a BOLO yet.' Sarge put his hands up to stop her protests. 'I said yet! We have no evidence your cousin or aunt have anything to do with Nick's dad's murder. Run the facial recognition though and if that falls short, I'll issue a generic statement that we are interested in any guests staying at William Creek who might have information regarding the death of Ron Johnston the owner.'

'Thank you Sir. I know it could draw unwanted attention.'

'You have no idea Williams. But we've stuffed too many poorly executed investigations into Manilla folders and buried them in the filing cabinet. I'll risk my career to make sure Nick gets the closure he deserves and if that means finding your missing family, well that will be a bonus.

Jenny wiped the corner of her eye with the back of her hand. Fighting back tears, and sniffed.

'Don't go mushy on me now Williams.' Sarge's eyes twinkled with unshed tears. 'Get on with it then.' He flicked his hand to shoo her away.

She jumped up. 'Yes Sir. Thank you Sir.'

'Don't thank me yet.'

# Chapter 23

A quiet focus hung over the police station. The cells were empty, the waiting room chairs sat abandoned, but the town was busy. With the cooler weather came busloads of tourists and grey nomads, caravanning their way across the country.

Coober Pedy was surrounded by iconic Australian tourist destinations. From the beautiful Flinders Rangers to the hot springs at Dalhouise, tourists travelled through the region on their way to Alice Springs and beyond.

But when the tourists were in town, everyone was prospering so the police, although on look-out for issues, weren't particularly busy with the locals. Bar fights and traffic violations were the most common issues they needed to deal with - except for two murders and three missing person's cases keeping everyone on staff busy.

Jenny's eyes wandered to the ledger sitting at the corner of O'Connell's desk where she left it earlier. The Senior Constable sat behind his computer monitor, peering through his chemist grade reading glasses at his screen.

She was desperate to break Pat and Ron's code, but her immediate case was Franny Kovac. She forced her attention back to the printout of three pieces of paper. The sum-total of a woman's life was in her hand.

*No.* She told herself. Franny's registration, licence and police record were only a small piece of her life. Who was she? What work did she do? Why was she back in Coober Pedy? Was cashing in on her deceased brother's estate the only reason?

'Sir?' Jenny waited for the Senior Constable to look over his glasses at her.

'What's up Williams?'

She waved the paperwork in the air. 'We know Franny Kovac came to town for the reading of Jason's Will, but we've not checked out her work history, her marriage history yet.'

'I've requested tax and bank records. That should answer her occupation and employer details. But you're right. We need to check if she ever married. Her only relative apart from Jason was her mother, now deceased, but she might have an ex we can talk to.' O'Connell rose from his desk. 'I'll leave you to it.' He waved her to take his seat. 'I need to grab some lunch anyway.'

'Thanks Sir.' Jenny slipped the paperwork in a folder on O'Connell's desk, before sliding into his seat. Getting access to Births Deaths and Marriages was usually a paperwork nightmare.

She needed to put in a request via email, marking it urgent due to extenuating circumstances. It had to be stamped and then signed by the Sergeant, and even then, it would take up to twenty-four hours to get a reply.

Fortunately, during their last murder investigation, Penny introduced her to Mack in records. He couldn't issue anything official, but he was at least willing to give her basic information over the phone.

'Don't forget to take a break.' O'Connell pulled his jacket from the back of the chair and put it on. The autumn breeze was particularly crisp.

'I won't Sir. I need to get Marj to identify a piece of jewellery we found in the debris anyway. And make sure she's okay.'

O'Connell studied her a moment, while she put her head down and searched for the contact information she needed for Mack at the Births Deaths and Marriages Registrar. She didn't notice the soft look in his eyes and the tiny curve of his lips.

His back was to her when she raised her head, ready to make the call. Pressing buttons, she dialled the number on the office phone and waited, tapping her fingers as the dial tone rang three, four, five times.

'Registrar's Office. Mack Sinclair speaking.'

'Mack. Hi. It's Constable Jenny in the bush.' She hoped he remembered her. It wasn't like they were best friends in school, although that would have been very handy. Jenny didn't keep in contact with many of her school friends. After Melanie disappeared, it became painfully obvious they were all only hanging out with her because she was the cool girl's cousin.

'Penny's friend. She told me you might call sometime.' His voice sounded breathy. 'Let me guess, you've got another *urgent* enquiry.'

She rolled her eyes. It must be super boring working behind a computer all day, filling out paperwork for attorneys and insurance companies.

'Well, technically this one isn't urgent Mack, but it is very close to home.'

'That's terrible. It's not a family member or anything?' His voice quavered with concern.

'Not my family Mack, but our lovely local motel owner had the gruesome discovery of her missing sister-in-law turning up murdered and hidden in the wall of her office.'

'Yuck, sounds horrible. She wasn't a fresh kill was she, that would be just….' She heard him gag. She didn't speak with Mack last time, Penny did, but she overhead the conversation and wondered about it at the time – but now, hearing Mack's dramatic tone, she understood why Penny played up to him so much last time.

'Oh thank heavens, no.' Jenny added a little drama to her own tone. Philips turned around, grinned, chuckled to himself, then returned his eyes to his own researching. 'It was still quite gruesome and well, I'd like to check on something to help us catch the killer and find some closure for our local, highly respected motel owner.'

'Of course Darl. What can I do for you?'

'I need to run a name for marriages, births, can you do that for me?' She held her breath.

'Of course. What's the name?'

Jenny gave Mack the details and waited while keys clicked on the other end of the line. 'Okay. Never married.' Jenny's heart sank. 'But....' More clicking told her Mack was adding search parameters.

'Got a birth certificate, no dad mentioned. DOB Nineteen, ninety-two. Twenty third March.'

Jenny wriggled in her seat, barely containing her excitement. 'Male or female?'

'Female. Only a single name given.' Jenny frowned. *Who registers a birth with just a first name?*

'Let me check something. Usually, when a baby is registered with one name, they are often stillborn?'

'Stillborn births are registered?'

'Yes Darl. If they are over twenty-one weeks, they aren't a miscarriage, they are newborn. But a death certificate will have followed the same day.'

Keys tapped as Jenny considered who decided twenty-one weeks was a real baby and twenty wasn't? How heart-breaking for the mums who never got a certificate of their baby's birth because they weren't close enough to full term.

'I've got a name change on her, but I can't release it Darl. I don't mind giving you something on a dead victim to help catch a killer, or notify next of kin, but this is a delicate one. Not worth risking my job over. You'll need a formal request. Sorry.'

'I understand totally Mack.' At least the baby's gender was revealed. 'And thanks so much for your help. Just one quick question, if you can.' She didn't wait for him to deny her. 'Was the name changed the year of birth or much later? Can you tell me that much?' She squeezed her hand tightly on the receiver and held her breath.

Mack hesitated. Jenny could almost hear him licking his lips. 'At birth Darl, but you didn't hear it from me. Okay?'

'Thanks Mack. I'll let you know when we catch the killer.'

'You do that.' Jenny hung up as Philips did the same on the counter phone.

'Sounded interesting.' He was still grinning.

'Mack, in the Registrar's office. Gotta meet him in real life when I get back to Adelaide sometime. I think he'll be a real scream.'

'No doubt.' He pointed to the phone. 'That was Penny. She called to say the ID is officially confirmed now. All the dental records matched and the coroner has signed off. We can't get a DNA sample, so that will have to do.'

'Well. I might just be able to find a DNA donor.' Philips eyebrows lifted. 'Not that we need one, but Franny had a daughter in March nineteen-ninety-two and put her up for adoption.' It was an educated guess, but it was the only sensible scenario she could gather from Mack's information.

'Well if she was put up for adoption, how can we get a DNA sample?'

'Because I have a hunch. But I need to grab some lunch to confirm.'

# Chapter 24

The Motel carpark hummed with activity, unusual for a Wednesday. Jenny passed a tourist bus parked outside the roped off reception area. The driver leant against the side, a smoke in his mouth, his mobile phone propped up close to his face, shaded, so he could see the screen with the bright sun overhead.

The bus was empty, no doubt a sign the occupants were going to be knee-deep at the bar ordering food. Jenny sighed. Maybe Niko's café was a better option for eating today, but she needed to speak with Marj.

Pushing the double glass doors open, she welcomed the cool air-conditioning. Despite the cool start, the day was heating up. The early desert wind had died off, leaving the sun pelting down on the dry, arid terrain.

Organised chaos reigned behind the bar with Stan, Kelly and Cheryl running around like a fire had broken out. Jenny scanned the room looking for Marj. The motel owner usually perched herself behind the Reception desk, but with the ongoing repairs, the woman was getting harder to nail down.

About to give up, a voice caught her attention. 'Officer. Can I help you?' Cheryl called from the bar. Jenny smiled. Since Tiffany's murder had been solved, Cheryl had slowly come out of her shell, but even in the thick of the investigation, the barmaid never called Jenny *Officer*.

Cheryl waved her over. 'Sorry about the formal stuff, but I didn't want an all-out brawl if I let you jump the queue. Let's just call it official business.' She winked and spoke sideways, her mouth twisted like a thief trying to sell her stolen goods.

'Got it.' Jenny scanned the sea of faces. One rounded man with a thin comb-over scowled at her. She pointed to the badge on her chest and he huffed, no doubt not buying the official business deal.

'I can wait for lunch Cheryl, but I do need to talk to Marj. Is she around?' Jenny cast her eye around the room again.

'She's out back, helping the cook.' Cheryl hoicked her thumb over her shoulder. 'The chef called in sick this morning.'

'Oh. I'll come back later.'

'Nah. Don't be silly. What's a few seconds going to hurt? Jump out the back and say hi. Grab a bowl of pasta while you're at it. You can fix us up later.'

Jenny's stomach grumbled at the thought of food. Cheryl lifted an eyebrow, just the one.

Her stomach was renowned in town already. There wasn't much Jenny didn't enjoy eating, but whenever she smelt food, her stomach habitually told everyone, very loudly, how hungry she was.

'If you're sure.'

'Go for it.' Cheryl pointed to the double doors clearly marked *IN* and *OUT*.

Jenny stepped cautiously toward the *IN* door. Entering, she was greeted with a hive of activity. The exhaust fan roared furiously, somehow matching the frenzied pace of movement. Steam wafted with the odour of garlic, onion and spices. Thick, dense, hot air pressed in around her.

Kelly rushed by, arms loaded with plates. Jenny ducked out the way, trying not to back into a stainless-steel bench full of plates laid out with salad, waiting for their allocated meal to be added.

Watching the scene made Jenny aware now wasn't the right time to be tearing Marj away from her work, but before she could retreat, the motel owner spotted her.

'Jenny. Luv. What can we do for you?' Marj waved her over.

'It's okay. I'll come back later.'

'Don't be silly.' She snatched up a plate of salad, rested it on her broken arm cast, then grabbed another and passed them to the cook who loaded a medium-rare rump on each. 'If this is about Franny. I want to know.'

Jenny drew a steadying breath. What she wanted to ask might be case related, but she wasn't sure if Marj was going to appreciate it or not.

'We've formally ID'd Franny. I'm so sorry for your loss.'

Marj stopped mid-stride on the way to collect two more garnished plates. Sighing, her shoulders dropped, but she perked up almost instantly. 'I was pretty sure luv, so it's no real surprise, but still…'

'She was your sister-in-law.'

'Exactly. And someone killed her. A terrible thought.'

'What did Franny do for a living?' Jenny decided to skirt around her main question for a moment. Six months earlier she would have gone in, all guns blazing, but Marj was a friend and her boss had taught her the importance of treading lightly with the locals.

'She was a freelance travel journalist.' Marj passed two more plates to the cook.

'Which magazines did she sell to?'

'Whoever would pay her the most.' Marj put all the recently loaded plates under the heat lamp ready for the serving staff. Sweat dripped from her forehead, her cheeks were flushed, but she rushed around seemingly unfatigued.

Marj wasn't afraid of a bit of hard work. Opal mining had brought her to the town. Meeting Jason had been fortuitous, a perfect match from all accounts, but it hadn't stopped the woman from working her guts out to get where she was.

'Marj?' The woman stopped at Jenny's tone.

'Spit it out luv.' She busied herself awkwardly tossing a load of fries out onto the stainless-steel trough and sprinkling them with ample salt.

'I did a little search.' She shrugged apologetically. 'I found records of Franny having given up a daughter for adoption, twenty-three years ago.' It wasn't strictly true. She was going on a hunch based on what Mack alluded to. 'Do you know anything about that?'

Marj held the salt container aloft, then put it down and turned to face Jenny. 'I knew. Jason handled the adoption for her. She was a mess.'

'Franny didn't do safe sex then?'

'Franny didn't do safe anything!'

'Why was she a mess? She wasn't exactly a teenager at the time.' Jenny's quick calculation told her the woman was over thirty, hardly a fragile teen mum.

'I don't know exactly, but the father wasn't on the scene. Franny was a traveller, drifting from place to place. I have no idea who she was pregnant to.' Marj averted her gaze. *She knew more than she was telling?*

'Do you know what happened to the daughter?'

'No. Like I said, Jason handled it all for Franny.'

'And he never told you who adopted the child?'

'No.' She rushed to the cool room, Jenny followed, but Marj was back out with a white plastic bag of pre-cut fries before she reached the door.

'I have to ask. You usually have a long list of theories when we have a curly case like this.' Jenny waited for Marj to make eye contact. 'Any hypothesis you think could help us? It's close to home, but we thought you'd be listing off ideas by the bucket load.' Jenny grinned, but Marj wasn't returning the gestures.

'I'm clueless when it comes to Franny.' She snatched her eyes away, seeming to busy herself with loading another batch of fries into the fryer, but Jenny could see the tension around her eyes.

'I've got a photo of a piece of jewellery, found in the debris in your office. Can you take a look at it?'

'Sure.' She relaxed, relieved at the subject change.

Jenny pulled up the photo on her phone, turned the screen and waited as Marj's eyes widened. She licked her lips, drew a few slow breaths, then made eye contact with Jenny.

'I thought I lost that years ago.'

Jenny frowned, searching Marj's face. 'It's yours?' She nodded. 'You're sure?'

'It's mine.'

The doors swung open. Kelly rushed in, arms full of dirty dishes.

'Service!' Marj called. 'Sorry luv. I better run now. It's peak hour out there. Grab a bowl of pasta on your way out.' She didn't wait for an answer. Her hands were already busy loading up plates from the warmer.

Jenny studied the earring photo, her mind racing. Marj's ears weren't pierced. Had they been five years ago? Or was she covering up for someone?

Either way, she was fairly certain she knew where Franny's daughter relocated to. It seemed so obvious. Marj not knowing was very unlikely, so why not tell the truth?

Still, she had no proof her theory was right. Not without a DNA test – and there was no probable cause to request one. So there was no point pushing Marj for more. Not yet anyway.

# Chapter 25

Jenny's hands flew to her hips at lightning speed. As much as she wanted to see the Sergeant's point of view, her gut was screaming at her that the Papadakis family was hiding something. Maybe it had nothing to do with Franny's death, but since Jenny was sure, almost beyond a doubt, that Tina was Franny's daughter, they at least needed to answer a few questions.

'Con Papadakis might as well be Mayor of Coober Pedy Williams.'

'But even if he were Mayor, this is a *murder* investigation. Questions need to be asked.' A bright red rash rose from her chest to her neck.

It had been months since she and Sarge argued over treading lightly with the locals. She understood why he wanted to be careful – she was delicate with Marj, but Con Papadakis was a big boy. He could handle a few questions.

'If Tina is Franny's biological daughter, then maybe Con or his wife had a motive to shut Franny up. Maybe she came back to town to get involved in her daughter's life.'

'Too many *ifs*. Get me some evidence. Con has already rung to complain you are badgering his family. I'm not sanctioning an interview with any of them. Unless you have questions about his staff, or the repairs, they are off limits. Got it Williams!'

'Got it Sir.' Jenny almost spat the words out, turned and strode from the Sergeant's office. She knew when she was beaten, but he hadn't warned her off entirely. She grinned. Sarge had given her the green light to keep digging, but where to go next?

She couldn't just wander up and ask Tina if she was adopted! Her thick wavy hair, and olive complexion matched the Papadakis family, but her height, build, hair colour and greenish hazel eyes were nothing like her parents.

Coober Pedy only had one school. Maybe she could check with teachers or friends of Tina's? If Tina knew she was adopted, her friends likely would too.

'Philips?' He glanced up as she leant in conspiratorially.

'What?' He scanned over her shoulder, a nervous look crossed his face.

'You went to Coober Pedy Area School, right?'

'There's only one school in town.' His tone was flat.

'I know, but some kids go away to boarding school, like Nick did.'

'The wealthy kids maybe. The rest of us plebs go to the local.'

She never considered Nick as being wealthy. He told her recently how hard it was surviving through the drought, but there was no doubt in her mind his parents would have made every effort to get him the best education.

Station kids were often sent away because they couldn't travel into town daily to get to school in any case, so if they had to board, they might as well board in the city.

'Did you know Tina Papadakis at school?'

'She's five years younger than me. The school's small, but I didn't pay too much attention to the younger kids.'

'Any older brothers and sisters? They're Catholic, aren't they? Don't most Catholic families have lots of kids?'

Philips shrugged. 'Stuffed if I know. If she has brothers or sisters, they are younger again because I don't know any of them.'

118

'So probably an only child.' Philips ignored the rhetorical questions, his eyes were already back on his computer screen. 'Want to come with me to question Tom again?'

His eyebrows rose. 'What's the plan?'

'I just want to ask him a few questions about Tina.'

'Nothing that's going to get me in trouble?' Philips waited for an answer. 'I heard Sarge yelling from out here. Stirring up trouble is a hobby for you Williams. You'll probably leave here once you solve your big family mystery,' he pouted. Philips might have been mildly offended she didn't tell him the truth, but this was new for him, 'but I'll be staying here. I like it here.'

'I get it Philips. I know you like it here.' It was beyond her understanding why. Philips could have a great career in the Police Force. When she first arrived in town, she assumed he was a slow, dim-witted country kid, but he proved her wrong, on numerous occasions. 'It's okay. I'll go alone.'

Philips shoved the computer mouse away, hard enough it hit the back of the counter and bounced. O'Connell glanced up from his desk, watched a moment, then returned his eyes to his own work. 'You can't go alone,' Philips whispered. 'It could be dangerous. Tom could be a killer.'

Jenny doubted it. She was going with or without his help and Philips knew it. But he was right. She was not being fair on him.

'Look, Sarge asked me to find proof Tina was adopted, and could be Franny's daughter before I could question the Papadakis family. I'm pretty certain this is the only way I'm going to get that proof – so by default, the boss knows about it and shouldn't get pissed off.'

'That sounds like a lot of assuming.' Philips rubbed his chin, then turned and stomped to his locker. Pulling it open

with more force than necessary, he grabbed his utility vest,
pulled it on and slammed the locker shut. Turning back to her
he huffed. 'You coming then!'

# Chapter 26

Ten minutes later, Philips parked the Police Landcruiser outside Tom's house. Nothing had changed, except this time, the tired hatchback was parked outside the garage and behind it sat a Vespa scooter in an unmistakably feminine shade of lilac.

'He's got company.' Philips adjusted his weapon as he stepped out of the driver's seat.

'Now we have to decide if we come right out and ask these questions head on or not.'

'Didn't Sarge say you couldn't question Tina?'

Jenny hesitated. *Is that what he said?* 'Kind of.'

'I don't like the sound of that.'

'I'll keep Tina talking. You ask Tom if he knows anything about Tina being adopted and warn him not to say a word to her if he says he does and she doesn't.'

'What are the chances of him knowing and not her?' Philips made a good point.

The front door opened as they approached, Tina's back appeared, she leant in to kiss Tom but he stopped her with his hand against her shoulder.

'Officers.' His voice was husky, his hair ruffled. Tina straightened her dress.

'Does your dad know where you are?' Jenny knew it was a cruel thing to say, aware of how her father felt about Tom, but she wanted to see the woman's reaction.

'Please don't tell him.' Her eyes misted over, her hands wrung against her chest.

'We won't.' Jenny held her hand out and gently touched Tina's arm. 'Is he really so overbearing?'

'You heard my mum. I'm promised and I'm supposed to be….'

'A virgin.' Jenny finished for her. 'My god Tina. You're a grown woman.'

'Please. Don't make a fuss.' She pressed invisible wrinkles from her dress with the palm of her hand.

'Has he threatened you?' Jenny could see Philips fidgeting next to her. He wasn't the confrontational type, but she knew the last thing he liked to hear about was treating women badly.

'No. Never. It's just…' They waited, but Tina shook herself before saying too much. 'I have to go. I'm sorry.' She rushed away so quickly, she didn't even stop to ask why they were at Tom's place.

Jenny watched his eyes chase her down the cracked concrete path to her scooter. The engine turned over and the little purple bike zoomed out of the driveway with an unexpected sense of urgency.

'What's going on Tom? Jenny rounded on the former tradesman.

'You heard her. She's promised.'

'Who to?'

'Alexi Samaras.'

'What the hell!' Philips shuddered. 'The guy has to be twice her age.'

'Is this a cultural thing?' Jenny fought the urge to put her hands on her hips.

'Maybe, but it's more a business decision I reckon.'

'What's that supposed to mean?' Jenny tapped her foot, her patience wearing thin.

'Look, it's not unusual, even these days, for arranged marriages to take place. It's not only a cultural thing, it's what rich families do all the time to secure business interests.'

Jenny got the distinct feeling Tom knew more about the subject than he was letting on. She made a mental note to do a search on his background when she returned to the station.

'Tina's managed to put the wedding off for years, but she's twenty-three now. There is no more waiting.'

'Why, what's so special about twenty-three?'

'It's all about heirs, isn't it? Fertility is ripe now, not in five or ten years.'

Jenny blew out her cheeks. 'That's barbaric.' Tom shrugged. 'Speaking of heirs.' Her gut rocked and rolled. How hypocritical would it be if Con's daughter was adopted? Another reason to put him on the top of her suspect list. If Franny threatened to share the truth, he could have killed her to keep her quiet.

'Do you know if Tina might be adopted?' Philips took over the questioning.

Tom laughed. 'Now that would be a thorn in the guy's side wouldn't it?'

'So Tina has never mentioned anything?' Philips wanted to be clear.

'Not to me. I doubt she knows either because if she did, why the hell would she do what her old man wanted, if he wasn't really her old man?'

Jenny wasn't so sure Tom was right. Tina seemed quiet, subdued and as angry as Mrs Papadakis appeared to be over her husband's marriage arrangements for their daughter, Jenny didn't see her standing up to the man.

'Why don't you two elope?' Jenny knew if it was her in the same situation, she would have.

'Because Tina won't break her mum's heart by splitting up the family.'

'Thanks for your time Tom.' Jenny excused them. Tom nodded, withdrew inside and closed the front door.

Philips shook his head in disbelief. Neither of them knew what to say. Jenny finally pulled herself together. 'Let's interview Alexi Samaras then. Who is he anyway?'

'The Mayor!'

'No way. How did I not know that?' Philips shrugged. 'I can see how an alliance between the Mayor and the largest builder in town could be advantageous. Dodgy land deals, guaranteed council contracts, environmentally questionable waste disposal.'

Jenny ticked off the points on her fingers as they wandered back to the police vehicle.

'Sarge is going to want to tread very lightly on this Williams.'

'Tell me about it, but if Franny found out something illegal was going on between her daughter's adoptive father and the local Mayor, that might be a reason to kill her.'

'That's assuming Tina *is* Franny's daughter.' Philips opened the driver's side door.

'Yes. I hope those adoption record comes through soon.'

'Me too, or we are still running blind with no motive.'

The police radio in the Landcruiser squelched as she opened the passenger's side. They rarely wore personal radio units unless on patrol for a major event. As soon as they left town, they didn't have the range anyway.

Police dispatch announced a disturbance. Jenny checked her phone. They had no reception, so O'Connell likely radioed dispatch. She picked up the handset.

'Five-five-seven responding.'

The radio squawked again as the despatch officer provided the details.

'That's Con's place right?' Jenny glanced at Philips as he turned the key on the V8 motor.

'It is.' He shoved the car into gear, did a U turn into the roadside verge, kicking up a veil of dust.

'Maybe Tina got back home and dad's not so happy?'

'I'm on it.' The vehicle hit 100 in record time. Jenny pressed the button to start the sirens and lights. She'd been in Coober Pedy nearly six months, and this was the first time she'd used all the bells and whistles. Tension tightened her muscles as adrenalin hit her veins.

# Chapter 27

The pounding in her chest was matched by the thudding in her ears as the Police Landcruiser sped toward the construction yard. No shots had been fired, but the caller indicated the situation sounded serious.

A small crowd of high-vis shirts gathered outside the office. Jenny clicked her seatbelt off and opened the door before Philips completely drew the vehicle to a stop.

Protocol dictated she wait for Philips before entering, but Tina's Vespa lay flat on the gravel carpark. The scene made her rush forward without thought for her own safety.

A woman's scream echoed from within. Concerned faces scanned one another. Jenny barged through the wall of onlookers. 'Police. Get out of the way.' She unclipped her weapon, but didn't draw it, instead, she lifted her taser and flicked the safety off.

'Right behind you!' Philips jogged up. 'Just take it slow.'

She nodded. 'Mr Papadakis!' A whimper carried through the office door. She couldn't see anything inside yet. The doorway was to the left of the entrance ramp. A male voice spoke in a warning tone, not loud enough for anyone outside to understand the words.

'Mr Papadakis!' Phillips tried. 'It's Constables Phillips and Williams. We are coming in.'

'Piss off and mind your own business.'

'We can't do that Sir. We've been called to a domestic incident and we can't leave until we have seen all parties are okay.' They waited outside the door. Con could be armed. They had no way of knowing what made the situation escalate so quickly to violence.

'Tina. Mrs Papadakis. Are you okay?' Jenny drew closer. Philips put his hand on her shoulder. She glanced around. He shook his head. He knew what she was thinking, but she had no choice. She needed to make sure neither woman was harmed.

'We are fine Constable.' Mrs Papadakis spoke tentatively, but clear enough for Jenny to hear.

'We are coming in Con. If you have a weapon, put it on the ground and put your hands in the air.'

'I'm not bloody armed. What do you think I am? This is only a family squabble. None of anyone's business.' Jenny stepped into the doorway as he spoke, her taser drawn and ready.

Con lifted his arms high when he saw the weapon aimed at him. Jenny scanned the room. Mrs Papadakis sat on a chair, her head in her hands, her shoulders shuddering. Tina cowered in the furthest corner of the room, her eyes wide, face flushed, tears running down her face. A nasty welt was already turning purple on her left cheek.

'We are going to have to restrain you Mr Papadakis.' Philips holstered his gun, clipped the sash closed and pulled a pair of handcuffs from his utility vest.

'What the hell for?'

'You've assaulted someone Mr Papadakis. You're under arrest.' He gaped at Jenny's response.

'It's family stuff,' he stuttered.

'Well Sir, family or not, it is illegal to strike someone. Even your daughter.'

'She won't press charges!' He glared at Tina.

'She doesn't have to. It will be up to the police prosecutor and personally, I'll be recommending he press charges.'

'You can't do that. I know the Mayor. He'll have your job.' He would have shaken his fist at her if it weren't already cuffed behind his back.

'I doubt it.' Philips grabbed Con by the shoulder and directed him out the front door.

'I need to take a statement.' Jenny turned to Mrs Papadakis first.

The woman shook her head, her eyes focussed on the hands in her lap.

'How long has this been going on?'

Another shake of her head, still no eye contact.

'You know he could kill one of you one day.'

The woman finally glanced up. She focussed on Tina, still hunkered down at the back of the office.

'He might have already killed someone.' She glanced from one woman to the other, hoping to see a reaction to the accusation. Nothing.

'I'll call for another car. You can both come down the station with me once we have Con in a cell.'

'He would never kill anyone.' Tina finally found her voice. 'He's just a little hot-headed sometimes.'

'And manipulative. And controlling. And a bully.' Jenny drew a quick breath to control her rising anger. 'He won't let you marry who you want. He wants you to marry someone twice your age. He hurts you when you don't do what he wants you to do.'

'You don't understand. He loves me.' She might actually believe those words.

'Tina.' She was about to ask about the adoption, but decided now wasn't the time and confirmation from the Births, Deaths and Marriages Registrar wasn't far away. 'Come down the station. Talk to me. I want to help you.'

Mrs Papadakis strode across the room with more confidence than Jenny expected from a battered wife. Wrapping her arm protectively around her daughter, she glared at Jenny. 'You can't break up our family.'

'She's a grown woman Mrs Papadakis. Tina will leave home eventually. Don't you want her to spend the rest of her life with someone who loves her? Not someone who wants to control her?'

Neither woman spoke. Mrs Papadakis drew herself up, wiped her face, wiped Tina's face and strode from the office, dragging her daughter by the arm. Jenny followed, hoping she'd gotten through to them, but instead of waiting for another police vehicle, they got into a navy-blue Lexus four-wheel drive and drove away, in the opposite direction from the station.

# Chapter 28

The interview room was cramped. Low ceilings and grey walls closed in around her; the smell of testosterone made her nose itch. O'Connell sat alongside her, focussed on setting up the recording equipment. Across the table, Con Papadakis scowled, while his lawyer babbled on with legal jargon.

Jenny nodded politely and waited for him to finish his rant. It seemed Alexi Samaras wasn't only the Mayor, and Tina's betrothed, he was a qualified lawyer who heard about Con's arrest before they even got him back to the station.

Jenny could only assume it was Mrs Papadakis who initiated the quick legal response. But why would the woman protect the man who slapped her daughter?

'You're new here Constable, I can see you don't know the run of things yet.' The lawyer's tone was condescending.

She'd heard enough. 'Mr Samaras.'

'*Mayor* Samaras.'

She lifted her eyebrows but amazingly held her tongue. O'Connell's lips curled. 'Mayor. You're here as Mr Papadakis's legal counsel, so we'll stick with Mr Samaras for now, unless of course you're playing a political card in a legal arena?'

Samaras' scowl now matched his client's. 'You have no witnesses. You have no case.'

'I heard the fighting as I approached the building Mr Samaras. I saw the distress with my own eyes.'

'Did you see anyone strike anyone else?' The lawyer was all calm, legal talk now.

She hadn't and he knew it. Everything was circumstantial. The assault charge wouldn't stick, but Jenny wasn't going to let this opportunity go.

'Mr Papadakis, I can understand hitting your daughter. Well, she's not actually your daughter, is she? She's adopted.'

'This line of questioning is irrelevant Constable.'

'Actually, it's interesting you should be here Mr Samaras. Aren't you promised Tina in marriage?'

Samaras puffed out his cheeks. His receding hairline glistened with sweat.

'I think we are done here. You're on a fishing expedition Constable and we aren't biting.'

'We have some paperwork to confirm Tina is adopted. Does she know?'

'You have no right to raise this with her.' Con lurched forward, his hands landing on the desk with a thud.

O'Connell's posture stiffened. A soft grunt left his lips and Con slid back into his chair, crossed his arms and sniffed, lifting his nose toward O'Connell.

'Tina is an adult. I'm waiting on confirmation from Births, Deaths and Marriages, but she's Franny Kovac's daughter, isn't she?'

'We are leaving!' Samaras pulled Con from the chair by the arm. His eyes scanned hers, then O'Connell's. He was more eager to leave the room than his client.

'You believe she doesn't know?'

'We never told her. My Selene couldn't have children.'

'You don't have to answer these questions Con. I strongly recommend against it.' The calm demeanour was evaporating.

'You and your wife went to a lot of trouble to adopt a child Con. Why are you hitting her and forcing her to marry this guy?' Jenny indicated the Mayor with her head. 'He's nearly twice her age.

'We are done!' This time Samaras didn't allow Con to stay seated. He clamped onto his arm with a vice-like grip, and dragged him from the chair so abruptly, the metal legs scraped along the lino floor. Once standing, he dragged him toward the door. In less than five seconds, Jenny and O'Connell found themselves staring at a blank wall.

'What the hell was that all about?' Jenny was stunned. Con was letting his guard down about his family, the adoption, everything, but his lawyer, the man betrothed to his daughter made it all stop. Why?

# Chapter 29

Philips opened his locker, put his utility vest away and pressed it closed.

'Let's call it a day people.' Sarge strolled out of his office, his mood lighter than Jenny expected given the interview they finished not long before.

'Somewhere to go Sarge?' O'Connell said the words Jenny had been thinking. In the last few months, her grumpy, stubborn, antisocial boss had become more cheerful, happy even.

'None of your business.' He rolled his lips to remove any hint of a smile. 'Good work today team.'

'We are still nowhere Sarge. No motive, no serious suspects. Just a lot of theories.' Jenny knew cold cases could take a while, but there were only a handful of people capable of hiding Franny in the motel office wall. Unless the plasterer was lying and the job wasn't partly done when he got there. But a background check didn't point to the plasterer having any reason to kill Franny.

'You'll get there Williams. I'm sure the penny will drop at some stage.' He lifted the front counter, left it open and strode to the exit. 'See you tomorrow.'

Jenny glanced from Philips to O'Connell. They were as stunned as she was. Not over Sarge knocking off early – that was common enough, but the lightness of his step, the hidden smile on his face. 'He's got a girl.'

'Absolutely.' O'Connell and Philips spoke in unison.

'You heading to the bar?' Philips asked as Jenny retrieved her backpack.

'No. I need to phone my brothers and then I'm going to dive into the code in Ron and Patricia's ledger.'

'You work too much Williams.'

'Nev and Tim are on night shift all this week and Nick is two hours away. I'm not exactly fighting off the party invitations.'

'You could have dinner with Dianna and me.'

Jenny smiled and touched her partner's arm gently. 'You know, that would be lovely but I really do need to talk to my brothers tonight and it could take hours. If Melanie ran away from home, I'm wondering if my older brothers noticed something I missed.'

'Don't give yourself a hard time. You were only seventeen when she went missing.'

'I know, but I get these occasional glimpses of events that make so much more sense if she actually did run away.'

'That's a good thing then, right?'

'Maybe.' She reached her car, pulled her keys from her pocket and opened the door. 'See you tomorrow.'

'See ya.' Philips waved as he got into his Landcruiser.

Ten minutes later she reached the dugout she shared with Nev and Tim. Parked outside was a Holden ute, complete with R.M. Williams mudguards and a longhorn sticker on the rear window.

As she locked her Dodge truck, a woman stepped out of the driver's seat. Fully expecting a tall, lanky cowboy, she was caught off-guard by a short, full busted woman wearing a floral dress and short cowboy boots. Her dark, wavy hair was pulled back in a low ponytail, her smile wide.

'Constable Williams?' Jenny was still in uniform and there was only one female cop in town. The answer was obvious, but she gave it anyway.

'Yes. Can I help you?'

'Can we talk inside?' The woman scanned the area. Her posture calm, her eyes wary.

'I'm not on duty.' Jenny wasn't keen to open their home up to a stranger.

'I might have information that could help your cold case.'

Jenny wasn't sure if the woman was referring to Franny or Ron's case, but either way, information was never unwanted, but why here, at her home?

'You could come down the station in the morning.'

'I could, but I won't. This town has ears and eyes everywhere.' She scanned her surrounds once more to highlight her concern.

'Can I at least ask who you are before I let you in?' Jenny stepped toward the front door, key in hand.

'I'm Nellie Patrick.' Jenny studied the woman. Her dark hair, deep brown eyes, broad nose and bronze skin spoke to her aboriginal heritage.

'Nice to meet you Nellie. Call me Jenny.' She opened the door. 'Come in.' The woman's demeanour made Jenny glance around before closing the door.

'I'm sorry to bail you up at home.'

'How did you find out where I live?' Her name wasn't on any lease. The property was supplied by South Australian Department of Health and they only knew Nev and Tim lived there.

'Nev told me. He said you wouldn't mind.'

'If Nev trusts you, that's good enough for me.' Jenny dropped her backpack on the breakfast bar and stepped into the kitchen. 'Can I get you a cuppa, wine, beer?'

'Beer would be great.' Nellie pulled out a bar stool. 'I do the occasional piece for the Coober Pedy paper, but I'm a freelance journalist slash blogger.'

Jenny retrieved two beers from the fridge, cracked the tops and handed one to Nellie.

'What can I do for you?' Jenny leant on the bar, not bothering to take a seat.

'Your cold case. I might have a way to contact witnesses.'

'What cold case do you mean? I'm working on a couple but one isn't exactly common knowledge.'

'Ron and Patricia Johnston.'

'How do you know about that case?' Her voice was laced with suspicion.

'Coober Pedy isn't very big Jenny. You exhumed Ron's body. Tongues started wagging. There had been rumours about their relocation program over the years, but his death being reclassified as murder, that got me very curious.'

'The murder hasn't officially been announced. I spoke to my boss the other day about a Crime Stoppers announcement, but he wasn't ready to do one yet. How did you find out about it?'

'Like I said. Coober Pedy is a small place.'

'Nev told you.'

Nellie sipped her beer to avoid answering the question.

'It doesn't matter. What have you got?'

'I write a blog, like I said. I wrote one recently about the murder case being opened and I got so may hits. A few in particular made me think they could have been part of the relocation program.'

'If they are all victims of some sort of abuse, they won't be coming forward anytime soon with information.' Jenny crossed the small kitchen to a pantry cupboard and pulled out a packet of potato chips.

'At least three comments were from people with ideas on who might have killed Ron.'

'The police don't usually take that type of thing seriously. Online comments are often from people trying to get attention.' She pulled the top open and passed the opened packet to Nellie who shook her head, her expression serious.

'The article mentions you Jenny.'

The handful of chips heading for Jenny's lips stopped mid-air. 'You named me?'

'I named all the officers on the team, but I did do a little focus article on your exploits since you got here. Three murders or suspicious death cases under your belt in less than six months. Very impressive.'

'Thanks, but I didn't ask for any attention and don't want it either.'

'Sorry, but you got it anyway. I got an interesting comment from someone who called herself Tinkerbell.'

The blood rushed from Jenny's head and the room began to waver. She dropped the chip packet on the bench, her snack forgotten. 'Tinkerbell. You're sure!' She leant on the corner of the breakfast bar for support.

'I'm sure. Does it mean anything to you?'

'It's what I called my cousin Melanie, because she was so small and pretty and the boys hung around her like the Lost Boys in Never Never Land.'

'Your cousin?' Nellie stopped with the beer-bottle halfway to her lips.

Jenny realised too late that Nellie didn't know about her personal stake in Ron's murder investigation.

'What did she say?' Jenny hurried on, hoping to cover her slip up.

Nellie frowned, her face lit up, ready to draw out more information, but she stopped herself. Jenny could see the cogs of her mind turning. 'She said Ron died a few days after she was relocated and maybe the person hunting her, killed him.'

'Did she say why she thought that likely?'

'No.'

'Why tell me?'

'Because Tinkerbell said you'd want to know.'

Jenny's heart fluttered enough to make her wonder if she were getting heart palpitations, but a few slow breaths stopped the sensation.

'Can you send her a message? Can you trace where she is?' Jenny's head was spinning. If Melanie was alive, and knew the killer, then she might still be in danger. But most of all, Jenny would give anything to hug her cousin again. To see her alive and well with her own eyes.

'Her comments were anonymous as far as no email or website or any avatar was provided. I guess with a forensic tech team I might be able to trace the IP, providing she wasn't using a proxy, but all I can do right now, with the expertise I have, is respond.'

'Can you respond with a message from me?'

'I can.'

'I'll write it down.' Jenny rushed around the kitchen, pulling drawers open, trying to find a piece of paper to write on.

'Here.' Nellie held out a spiral notepad and pen. 'Use this.'

# Chapter 30

Philips leant against the front counter, taking a report of a missing dog. Jenny sipped her cold coffee as O'Connell wandered out of Sergeant Mackenzie's office.

A woman in her late fifties entered the foyer. Her skirt rode well above her knees, her white blouse hung low, revealing cleavage and the six-inch wedged heels she wore made her totter like an unstable toddler.

'Hiya boys.' She noticed Jenny. 'And girls.' Her bright white teeth were perfectly aligned. 'I hear you might have a story for the paper. Or at least a statement.'

'Gwen. Nice to see you.' O'Connell approached the counter, nodding to Jenny that he'd handle the visitor.

'Oh John, if only you meant that,' she swooned.

*John.* Jenny leant out and around O'Connell, pulled a face in Philips' direction, but he was too busy chuckling under his breath to respond. She'd never heard O'Connell's first name before. Come to think of it, she didn't know Sergeant Mackenzie's either. Raising her eyebrows to her partner, she mouthed the word *John* with fluttering eyelashes. He scoffed, O'Connell glared, Philips averted his gaze, then scoffed again.

'Gwen. You know we contact the paper if we have a statement to make.'

'I can help John. You need a lead. I know you do. I can run a story, asking for anyone who saw Franny leading up to the murder to contact you.'

'And you wouldn't be embellishing the story or adding a layer of tabloid crap to boost your advertising in the process?'

Gwen placed her palm on her chest. Deadly looking bright red acrylic nails splayed out and tapped up and down. 'You wound me.'

'Who have you lined up to go on the same page as the article? Let me guess? The new craft beer brewery. Or the roof restoration guys. They'd benefit from exposure around a murder case which destroyed the front of the building. Or maybe Con has offered to run a big spread to boost your income stream?'

'That's not fair John,' Gwen pouted. 'I need advertising to pay the bills. I can't put only news in the paper or there wouldn't be a dollar to spend on printing the bloody thing.'

It seemed the Senior constable had hit the nail right on the head.

'Righto Gwen. I'll give you a few lines.' Sergeant Mackenzie strode from his office. 'Just a few lines, that's it. I'm sure you've got enough gory photos of the crime scene to fill the pages.'

'The more you give me, the less I have to make up.' Gwen's eyes challenged Sarge.

'Ok, get your pen out.' Gwen did as she was told. 'The body of Franny Kovac was discovered amongst the debris of the motel office crash on Saturday May sixteen. It is believed she met with foul play, although we are awaiting a full autopsy report from the coroner in Adelaide.'

Gwen scribbled in a mix of short-hand and full writing.

'At this stage, we appeal to anyone who may have seen Franny Kovac – I'll give you a photo before you go – in and around the *Opal Inn Motel* on Wednesday the twenty-third of June two-thousand and ten.'

'Are we going to get one of those re-enactments?' Gwen's whole body quivered with excitement.

'I don't think so Gwen.' Sarge retrieved a photo of Franny and passed it over the counter. 'Now if you fill that article with a heap of crap, it will be the last statement I give you Gwen. Got it!'

'Got it Sarge.' Gwen flipped her notepad closed, collected the photo from Sergeant Mackenzie's hand and winked at O'Connell before turning on her heel and striding, as best she could with the shoes she wore, out the front door.

'Who the heck was that?' When no one answered, Jenny glanced around to find all three men focussed on the tightly wrapped butt strutting out the door.

'That my dear was O'Connell's ex-wife.' Sarge chuckled, turned and wandered back to his office leaving Jenny opened mouthed. Philips giggled like a school kid and O'Connell blushed. Something she'd never seen him do.

She often wondered if O'Connell ever married. Now she knew. Maybe Gwen was what kept the cop in town. He should have been running his own station by now, but it didn't look like they were still in love with each other.

There was something else keeping the Senior Constable in Coober Pedy and she was keen to find out, but not now. Now she had two cold cases to solve.

Jenny returned her attention to decoding the ledger. Although she took it home last night, Nellie's visit left her unfocussed. The evening was a waste as she agonised over whether Melanie would reply to Nellie's message.

In the end, she called Nick to debrief. The homestead was coming along. They'd be another few months, but she was keen to get out and see the progress on the reconstruction of the beautiful old sandstone mansion.

Sam was coming back from his travels in the next month or so, but Nick, for the first time ever, seemed lonely on his own out on the station. Sure, the workmen were there during the week, but without Sam, Nick was alone. She wanted to spend more time there, but her job was in town, over two hours away.

Shaking herself, she focussed back on the ledger and ran the cipher she planned on trying over the last few pages.

The only way she was going to know if the cipher was right would be if she identified Melanie and Aunt Carolyn's names with each decoding. Since Ron died shortly after Melanie was seen by the stockman Ed on the William Creek property, it stood to reason her name would be amongst the last few entries.

She wanted to try the basic A1Z26 option, where 1 = A and 26 = Z, but the ledger had few if any numbers in it. It was all alphabetical gobbledygook. So she tried the Rot13 Cipher. Where each letter of the alphabet was run in a line of 13, A – M were 1 – 13, then Z – N ran backwards below them, then they were transposed. Making H a U and vice versa.

She had no access to any fancy computer program to run the cipher, but she quickly scanned the last few pages for the letter Z, since M transposed to Z, a Z would be easy to find. She found a few, but only one listing Z.J. or M.W before the cipher.

This was the entry she was looking for. Now to figure out how the dates were encoded.

No matter what combination she came up with, nothing translated to dates. She re-read the same line so many times, it became clear her brain wasn't absorbing anything anymore.

She needed to take a break. Too much time focussing on one thing often sent her mind elsewhere. Or was she hungry? Being low on energy could mean she needed food.

Sarge's words flooded into her mind. *Franny Kovac's case is our priority. Don't let the ledger get you side-tracked.*

Shaking her head back into the game, she typed Tom Hammond's name into Facebook and the internet browser, selecting images, then waited for something to populate.

The browser screen slowly filled with photos. It was hard to be sure, because Tom wore a long beard and daggy jeans, but the face peering back at her looked like the same man.

Tom Hammond was the son of a mining magnate. The papers in Adelaide had gone crazy. Articles were in all the tabloids and women's magazines. References to his failed engagement to the daughter of a major department-store chain owner were plastered over every piece of media for nearly six months after the engagement was called off.

'How did Tom go to school with Tina if he was the son of a mining giant?'

'What was that?' Philips answering her rhetorical question made her aware she spoke aloud.

'Tom Hammond is heir to a fortune.'

'What!' Philips frowned.

'Can we check the Coober Pedy school records for Tom Hammond?'

'I'll call now.' Philips lifted the office phone and dialled.

Jenny focussed on the screen, put her fingers on the keyboard and began to type. She was a good typist, but occasionally, when she was swapping from one keyboard to the other, she had to realign her fingers on the keys. As she studied the keys now, she nearly slapped her forehead.

Was it that easy? Had it been in front of her all along?

Testing her theory, she opened the ledger and scribbled down some numbers.

'Yes!'

'What?' O'Connell glanced up from the desk.

'The code. I've broken the ledger code.' She fist-pumped the air as Philips hung up and frowned at her. His odd expression spoke volumes. She blushed, put her hands in her lap and waited for him to speak.

'No one by the name of Tom Hammond attended Coober Pedy Area School.'

# Chapter 31

All four of the team crowded into Sergeant Mackenzie's office. The whiteboard showed Franny's case facing out. Jenny fought the urge to rush straight to her decoding of the ledger and spin the board around to Ron's murder case, but she needed to focus on solving Franny's murder first.

'Tom Hammond, the chippy who worked on Marj's office is actually connected to big money.' Jenny scribbled the details onto the board. 'Selene Papadakis claimed Tom was a school friend of Tina's, maybe that's what she told her mum.'

'When did they meet?' Sarge leant back in his chair, his left index finger tapped his top lip.

'We haven't asked them. It didn't seem relevant.'

'Maybe it isn't, but then again, we now know Franny was Tina's mother. The adoption papers came through.' O'Connell snatched the whiteboard marker pen from Jenny's hand and wrote the details down, using a piece of tape to add a copy of the record to the board.

'But we still don't know who the father is.' Jenny stepped back to study the board.

'We still don't have a motive.' Philips leant against the doorway, his eye on the front counter.

'Marj told me Franny was a travel journalist. Sold her stories to anyone who would pay for them. Maybe this is about the Mayor and Con being up to something, doing deals? Maybe she didn't like the idea of her adopted daughter being married off in an arranged marriage to a man twice her age.'

Jenny wasn't sure this was motive for murder, but it would have made her angry if she were Franny and found out about it. She carried on theorising. 'The reading of Jason's Will could have brought her to town, but maybe she checked up on her daughter while she was here? Or maybe she smelt a story?'

The main phone rang. Philips left the office to take the call.

'She was a travel journalist, not an investigative reporter. Maybe she wanted to catch up with a boyfriend.' O'Connell shrugged when Jenny frowned at him. 'Just a thought.'

'I showed Marj the earring. She recognised it. Said it was hers, but her ears aren't pierced. Were they pierced five years ago?'

'You're asking the wrong people.' Sarge chuckled. 'Jewellery isn't exactly our thing.'

'Actually. They weren't. I would have noticed.' O'Connell answered. Sarge pulled a strange face. O'Connell rolled his lips like he wished he'd said nothing.

'We know it wasn't Franny's or at least a matching one wasn't found with her body. So whose earring was on the scene? And why is Marj lying about it?'

'I don't want to badger Marj about it yet.' Sarge studied the whiteboard as Jenny put a picture of the earring on it and made notes with a link to Marj's details.

'We couldn't hold Con. Is there any history of abuse?' Jenny studied the faces. Everyone shook their head. 'Why would he go to the trouble of adopting a daughter, then treat her badly?'

'Leave him be for now Williams. The Mayor is breathing down my neck, threatening to raise allegations of police harassment.'

'That sets off alarm bells right there.' O'Connell retrieved the pen from Jenny's hand, added the Mayor's details to the board. She grinned, but turned to see Sarge not sharing her amusement.

146

'Franny is dead. I'll see if I can get a judge to open the adoption records. See if the Papadakis family did adopt her.' Sarge picked up his phone.

'I'll call Penny and check the other earring didn't turn up in the debris, but I'm sure she would have called if it did.'

'You do that.' O'Connell followed Jenny toward the main office. Philips met them at the door. 'Just got an anonymous caller who said they saw the article in the paper.'

'Already!' Jenny wished they had made an announcement earlier. Sarge could be so stubborn.

'Apparently. They said they are a regular at the motel and noticed an unusual vehicle parked up the road around that time.'

'How unusual can a car be parked near the local watering hole?' O'Connell seemed ready to dismiss it as he dodged between them and crossed the room to his desk.

'They said it stood out because it was a really *posh* one.' Philips used air quotes over the word *posh*.

'Posh. And they didn't leave a name?' O'Connell was suddenly interested again.

'No, but there aren't many regulars at Marj's place. She might be able to work out who our tipster is.'

'Who cares who they are. We just need to know what *posh* car they saw and if they got a registration number.' Jenny rushed to the counter computer, her fingers hovered over the keyboard, her eyes questioning Philips.

'They didn't know the exact make. Said it was one of those huge monster trucks with all the fancy extras. I quizzed them with a few models. F-250, Raptor, that type of thing.'

'Any guesses which model?'

'He wasn't sure but there weren't too many around town five years back. It's too long ago for us to get footage from our cameras. We don't keep it that long and there is no guarantee it was parked within our station camera range. Leave it with me, I'll run a few makes and models through the system and see what pops.'

Philips joined her at the counter.

'Okay, thanks.' She stepped away to give him room. 'I forgot to tell Sarge. I think I've cracked the code to the ledger.'

'That's great.' Philips was only half listening as he typed details into the computer.

'I'll be back in a minute.' She scurried to Sarge's office. The door was still open and saw him hang up from his call.

'Sir. I almost forgot. I think I've found the cipher for the Johnston ledger. Can I send it to the techs to get it fully decoded?'

Sarge sat back. 'Good news. Get them to focus on the last year's entries. They won't have time for anything else.'

'Will do Sir. Did we get a warrant?'

Sarge nodded. 'Records are on their way.' Jenny turned. 'Williams!' She stopped and turned back. 'Did you find your cousin's details in the ledger?'

'Yes Sir. It was her name that helped crack the code.'

'We'll find her.' Sarge's expression grew serious.

'Actually Sir. A blogger named Nellie contacted me yesterday. I've got nothing concrete, so I didn't update the case notes yet, but she ran a story on our investigation.'

'Bloody bloggers and would-be journalists.'

'It was bound to happen.' O'Connell's voice made Jenny jump.

'You're as silent as a ghost.' Something about the lift of O'Connell's lips made Jenny curious. She was about to ask a question, but the sound of her boss huffing as he composed himself made her stop.

'Sir, Nellie believes a few of the relocated victims responded to her blog. One of them used a nickname I gave Melanie. She might be one of them. I asked Nellie to post my reply. Fingers crossed she gets it.'

'No tangents Williams. Update the board with what you know.' Sarge pointed to the crime board.

'I'll phone Penny, send the ledger off, then do it Sir.'

Jenny's stomach fluttered in a comfortable, happy kind of way. She was getting the hang of the whole teamwork thing. Working behind Philips and Sarge's back created more tension than she realised. She might not always see eye to eye with her boss, but having the investigation out in the open lifted a heavy load off her chest.

If only her family were as relieved as she was over the police officially getting involved. The fact they were annoyed still concerned her. But what they thought didn't matter anymore. Melanie might be alive and better yet, she might be able to get in contact with her.

Jenny dialled the Adelaide lab and waited.

'Forensics. Penny speaking.'

'Just the person I wanted to talk to.'

'Jenny. What's up?'

'I decoded the ledger.'

'That's fantastic.'

'And there's more, but I need to ask something about our current case first.'

'Don't leave me hanging.'

'Did you find another earring in the debris?'

'Nope. Just the one.'

'Anything else we didn't already know?'

'No. Whoever wrapped the victim in plastic wore gloves or the oils deteriorated over the years. There were no prints or DNA. I narrowed down the nail gun models, based on nail size and the year. I'll send you the list, but whoever had the tool has probably replaced it by now. They don't have a long lifespan in commercial use. Five years is a long time in a tradesman's tool's life.'

'Thanks Penny. I'll check it out.'

'What about the ledger?' The genuine excitement in Penny's voice made it difficult for Jenny to breathe.

Taking a deep breath, she forced herself to focus. 'Melanie might be alive Penny.' She explained about Nellie.

'That's awesome. You might finally finish up your family case and be able to come back to the big smoke.'

A knot formed in Jenny's stomach. Did she want to go back to the city? Never living through another dry, hot summer in the red centre of the country was appealing, but leaving her new friends behind. Leaving Nick. Her stomach did a summersault.

'Too early to get my hopes up.'

# Chapter 32

Philips fidgeted next to her, obviously anxious for her to end her call with Penny. The twinkle in his eye told her he found a lead while running vehicles through the registration office.

She dropped the handset onto the desk phone and turned. 'You'll never guess who owned an F-250 twenty ten model back in June twenty-ten.'

'Did own? They sold it?'

'Yeah, I did a current registration search and found a few fancy utilities in town, but none owned by anyone in our suspect pool.' He rubbed his chin. 'I thought to myself, *What would Williams do?* and I ran an historical check.'

'Nice work. Who owned a brand-new F-250 back then?' She could see the excitement on his face.

'Guess.'

'Come on Philips.' She didn't want to play games.

'Sorry. Mayor Samaras.'

O'Connell entered part-way through their conversation. He fixed Philips with a stare. 'What's that about the Mayor?'

'It was *his* car parked up outside the motel the night Franny was killed,' Philips explained.

'I might have put him on the board but we can't simply rock up to the Mayor and accuse him of killing Franny Kovac. You'll both need to dig for a motive.'

'Do we have Franny's financials yet?'

'No. I'll chase them up.'

'You said you did a search and none of our suspects owned a big, pimped out utility, but we can see who owns the vehicle now. They might know something.' Jenny pointed to the computer Philips had been using. He grinned, then hit *print* on the file he found.

'Tread lightly.' O'Connell pointed to Jenny.

'Me?' Jenny touched her chest. 'I always do.' Philips laughed. O'Connell chuckled under his breath.

'You get results Williams, but treading lightly isn't in your nature.'

Jenny crossed the room to her locker, retrieved her utility vest and pulled it over her head. Philips joined her.

'I'm amazed the car is still in town. If the Mayor did anything that night, then sold the car to cover it up, why sell it locally?' Jenny signed her pistol out, guided it into her holster, then snapped the tab shut.

'He wanted to move it quickly I guess.' Philips collected the Police Landcruiser keys and strode toward the door. Jenny followed.

Ten minutes later they pulled up outside an industrial shed on the outskirts of town, not far from Con's business premises. The vehicle was parked in front of a massive shed, the roller door open, a yellow mining truck occupied the bay.

They stepped out of the Police vehicle. Jenny donned her Akubra to keep the sun at bay. They circled the F-250 truck, not sure what they expected to find after all this time.

'Officers?' A tall, lean man in his late fifties with a thick black moustache and even thicker eyebrows approached them. 'What can I do for you?' A forced smile thinned his lips.

'Dragan Jovanovich I assume?' Jenny glanced past the man to see a woman scurry from his office, her head down, hastily adjusting her dress.

Dragan cleared his throat. Jenny's eyes returned to his. 'We just have a few questions about the purchase of this vehicle.'

'I've had it for nearly five years now, is there a problem?'

'Not necessarily. We understand you purchased the vehicle from Alexi Samaras.'

'Yes. I know him through our membership with the Coober Pedy Business Association. I've known Alexi for years. He wanted to move the car on, I agreed to buy it.' He shrugged. 'Is there an issue?'

Jenny found the flood of unprompted information unusual. She glanced at Philips, who didn't seem concerned.

'Can we take a look at the vehicle?' Philips asked as he tried the door. It was locked.

'I don't see why not, but I'd appreciate it if someone would tell me what this is all about.'

'This vehicle was seen parked outside the *Opal Inn Motel* on the night of Franny Kovac's murder.' Jenny watched his face carefully, hoping to see a reaction. Nothing. Not even a touch of sympathy.

'Heard about that. Nasty business. But I fail to see how a car parked outside the motel causes the Police any concern.'

'Considering the Mayor and yourself aren't frequent patrons of the motel bar and restaurant, we did find it an unusual location to find the vehicle parked.' Philips pulled his notepad out. 'Where were you on the night of Wednesday twenty-third June twenty-ten?'

'I didn't buy the vehicle until Friday the twenty-fifth.'

'That seems very specific Mr Jovanovich.' Jenny locked eyes with him as he rolled his lips together and averted her gaze.

'I'm good with dates.'

'Then you'll remember where you were that evening,' she coaxed. The registration office change of ownership backed up his story about buying the vehicle on the twenty-fifth, but it could easily have changed hands earlier and they agreed to lie on the documentation. Maybe they were covering for each other?

The vehicle could be an elaborate way of providing an alibi for the murder should the body ever be discovered. But still, Jenny wondered why anyone built like the Mayor or Jovanovich would need to hide the body in the wall of Marj's office. It was the same issue she had understanding why Con would.

'My wife and I were out. I was rapt to pick up the F-250 at such a bargain price and splashed out on a nice dinner at the Big Winch.'

'All out indeed.' Jenny scoffed. The bar and grill was popular with tourists. It did have a great sunset view, but she hardly considered it *splashing out*.

'Did you know Franny Kovac, Mr Jovanovich?' The question she'd been dying to ask got the reaction she was hoping for.

Dragan's eyes widened, squinted, then shut completely as his face rolled through various emotions. One appeared to be genuine sadness.

He sniffed, drew a breath, then blew it out slowly. '*Everyone* knew Franny Kovac.'

Jenny glanced at Philips. 'Just how *well* did you know Franny?' The woman tugging her dress back down as she scurried from the office flicked into Jenny's mind. 'She was in town for her brother's Will reading, but she adopted a child out in nineteen-ninety-two.'

Dragan opened his mouth to speak, but closed it and shook his head.

'I think you'll need to speak to my lawyer if you have any further questions.'

'Let me guess. Mayor Samaras is your lawyer?' Jenny rolled her eyes.

# Chapter 33

Philips climbed into the driver's seat, closed the door and watched Dragan Jovanovich stroll back into his office.

'What do you make of that?' His eyes followed the figure until he disappeared inside.

'I think he knows something. Let's see if Franny's bank and credit card records have come through yet.'

'I get dibs on running these guys through police records.' Philips turned the key to start the engine.

'I doubt they have records unless they go back to juvenile days, but worth a check. If anyone had any dirt on Samaras, surely he wouldn't have made Mayor. I'll see if anyone else with the Business Association looks like a person of interest.' Jenny clipped her seatbelt on as Philips backed the vehicle out of the mechanic's industrial lot.

'We still don't have a motive.'

'Other than the adoption, which we are sure was Tina, we have nothing. I'll try to convince the boss to let us interview her. She's an adult. If she doesn't know, she should.'

'That's not our job to share that information.'

'It is if it's pertinent to our case.'

Philips glanced at her before pulling out onto the road and heading back to the police station.

They drove past Con's yard on the way back, slowing to check there were no disturbances like yesterday.

'Can we call past the Papadakis's house?'

'I don't think that's a good idea.' Philips glanced at her, then put his eyes back on the road.

'No,' Jenny sighed. 'You're probably right, but I hate this waiting. Waiting on forensics, waiting on adoption records, waiting on bank records and more evidence so we can question the Mayor, Con, even Tina properly. I've got a gut feeling they are all linked in this.'

'Fingers crossed we'll have some bank and phone records to go through when we get back.'

'I hope so.' Her brow furrowed, making her think of something her granddad used to say about the wind changing and being stuck like that. Philips must have noticed her expression.

'You look like you need coffee,' Philips grinned.

'Great idea.'

A few minutes later Philips drew the Police Landcruiser up outside Niko's café. Jenny hopped out, Philips stayed in the car. Pulling the screen door open, Jenny spotted Selene and Tina Papadakis huddled together in the corner.

Tina's eyes were red rimmed. Her mother's arm was wrapped around her shoulder. Jenny tried not to stare, but failed. Niko's voice drew her attention, making her jump.

'What will it be today Officer Jenny? Your usual?'

'Yes thanks Niko, all four usuals.' She wasn't sure if Sarge and O'Connell would want coffee this late in the afternoon, but it felt rude not to take them one each.

'On it now. Won't be a moment.' Niko stepped across to the large, six cup machine with antique looking glossy copper coloured paint and polished chrome.

Jenny strained to hear the quiet conversation between the two women, but Selene noticed her eavesdropping. Shuffling her chair around, she put her back between Tina and Jenny.

*Busted!* Tina appeared too distraught for Jenny to mind her own business. Strolling over, she stopped between the two women 'Mrs Papadakis. Tina. Are you okay? Anything I can help with?'

Tina sniffed, blew her nose on a tissue and remained silent. 'We are fine thanks Officer. Just girl talk. You know how it is.'

'Is it about Tom?' Tina's eyes fixed on Jenny's. She resisted the urge to pull out a chair and take a seat. It was obvious she wasn't invited. 'Did you know he was the son of Hammond Mining?'

Tina's eyes grew wide, but it was Selene Papadakis' reaction that caught her eye. Her mouth gaped open, then her expression evened out. Neither woman spoke.

'Selene, you told me Tina went to school with Tom. Was that a lie, or did you not know how they met?'

'Officer. I'm sorry but we can't be talking with you without a lawyer present.'

'Is that what your husband told you?'

Tina wiped her nose again. As she turned to toss her tissue in a bin nearby, Jenny noticed a delicate, intricately patterned gold pendant hanging around her neck. Tina saw her eyes on the necklace, and buried it quickly below her collar.

'I'm going to come right out and ask you both a question. I'm sorry if its offensive and I fully understand if you decide to make a complaint to my boss, but I think it needs to be brought out into the open if not already.' Jenny drew a deep breath, ready to ask the burning question on her lips.

'Coffee's up Constable.' Jenny turned to see Niko holding up a tray. She waved, then turned her eyes back to the women, in time to see them shuffling from their seats.

Jenny put her hand on Mrs Papadakis' arm, holding it gently. The woman glared at her grip.

'Does she know?' Jenny asked. Mrs Papadakis frowned, then realisation hit her.

'Let's go Tina. Now!'

*Take that as a no!*

Jenny watched them leave; the screen door swung shut with a loud thud. As she turned to collect her coffee order, she noticed the tissue in the nearby bin.

'Niko, can I please grab a spare paper bag?'

# Chapter 34

'I told you it wouldn't go well.' Philips was berating her for the tenth time since she told him about her conversation at Niko's café.

'I shouldn't have told you.'

'Told him what?' O'Connell peered over his glasses as they entered the back of the station.

Jenny approached, put his coffee on the desk. 'Hope you wanted one? Wasn't sure. Figured I should get you one in case.'

'Thanks.' His eyes drilled into hers. 'What shouldn't you have done?'

'I bumped into Tina and Selene Papadakis at Niko's.' She strolled toward Sarge's office without a backward glance.

'He's not in.' O'Connell spoke. 'What shouldn't you have done?'

'It's nothing. I didn't even actually ask.' O'Connell's stare dug into her like a knife. 'Okay. I asked if Tina knew yet. I didn't say what, I simply alluded to, you know, the adoption and Mrs Papadakis couldn't get out of Niko's café fast enough so I'm guessing that's a *No*!'

She knew she'd done the wrong thing, but the pace of this case was slower than Nick's dad's murder and her insides were screaming at her to get the ball rolling.

Agitating the Papadakis women was probably not her best idea yet, but it worked. She now knew Tina either didn't know, or at the very least, no one had ever told her she was adopted.

*Unless Franny did!*

'Sir, before you haul me over the coals.' She looked over her shoulder at Sarge's office. 'Or worse, tell Sarge, I think I have a possible motive for Franny's murder. I also managed to get Tina Papadakis's DNA.' She waved the tissue bag in the air.

'I don't want to know how you got that.'

'It was out in plain sight Sir.'

O'Connell removed his glasses from his nose, placed them on the desk, then rubbed between his eyes where a red indent sat. Picking up his coffee, he deliberately drank slow sips, obviously composing himself. O'Connell rarely lost his temper. She'd only seen him raise his voice once, during a police interview, and even then, she was certain it was all show.

'Give me your motive theory then.'

'If Franny told Tina she was adopted. That she was her daughter...'

'We don't know that yet.'

'Well we have the DNA now to confirm.'

'Do you know how long DNA sampling takes on a case like this?'

'I'll check to see if the adoption records are through yet. But I think I'm right. If I am, then would finding out make Tina want to kill her mum for giving her up?'

'I think that's a pretty weak motive for murder.'

'I'm sure the birth, or adoption have something to do with it. Did we get Franny's bank and phone records yet?'

'What do you think I was doing when you came in?'

Jenny peered around the computer at O'Connell's desk. Piles of printouts were splayed all over it.

'These are the phone records from back then.' He picked up a wad of paperwork. 'And this is her bank records.' Another pile appeared in his hand. 'Who wants which?' His eyes scanned their faces.

'I'll take the money,' Philips offered.

'I'll run the numbers.' Jenny grabbed the wad from O'Connell's left hand. Philips stepped up for the pile in his right.

Jenny pulled up a stool near the front counter computer. She might need to search phone numbers to see who Franny called around the night she was killed.

Philips thumbed his way through his pile next to her. A pink, yellow and green marker pen at the ready. She saw him circle figures, then move on.

Jenny had a head for numbers, if she knew what she was looking for. But finding call patterns on a piece of paper from the telecommunications company without a reference starting point was hard.

She mulled over her suspects. Tina, Selene and Con were all prime if Franny's death had anything to do with the adoption. There was still the chance Franny died because of some investigative article about Con, the Mayor and maybe even Dragan being involved in dodgy dealings, and she couldn't rule out that Franny was contesting Jason's Will. Marj was still a suspect.

The murder occurred on her property, after an altercation. She shook her head. Marj wasn't a killer, but then again, Philips didn't believe Len Holmes could cover up murder either.

She dismissed the thought and focussed on the victim. Franny liked to travel. She liked her relationships unencumbered. The Mayor's car was seen parked near the motel the night of Franny's death. Not in the carpark where you'd expect, but down the road. Maybe Franny was sleeping with the Mayor?

Then there was Dragan, who said he got the vehicle after Franny died, but registration paperwork could be purposefully delayed. She needed to check his alibi, but doubted anyone would recall if he was out for dinner with his wife nearly five years ago.

Finally, she needed to consider Tom Hammond. He was a tradesman. If Tina was involved in Franny's death, then Tom might have helped cover it up. She couldn't see him having any other motive for being involved. Either way, she ran his mobile number too.

Five minutes later she held a printed list of everyone's mobile, business and home numbers. Putting the list alongside the communication printouts, she started to scan. Like Philips, she wielded different colour marker pens. After a few minutes of circling numbers, it became obvious she was going to need more colours.

Franny's phone records showed she spoke to all but one suspect the few days leading up to her death. Tom was the only number not popping up.

'Damn!'

'What's up?' Philips glanced over.

'Every single suspect was in contact with Franny in the few days before she died.'

'Drill down to Wednesday afternoon and evening only.' O'Connell called from the other side of the room.

'On it Sir.'

'I've got something. Well, I think I have.' Philips waved a piece of paper in the air.

'What is it?' O'Connell rose from his chair and circled round the desk. Stepping up behind Philips. He peered over his shoulder.

Jenny abandoned her paperwork to join them.

'See these deposits?'

Jenny and O'Connell nodded.

'This amount is deposited into Franny's account three times, at the beginning of each month.'

'What dates have you got there?' O'Connell adjusted his reading glasses.

'These go back from the murder to January twenty-ten Sir.'

'I'll request records further back.' O'Connell strode to the desk, picked up the phone and began dialling.

'How many years can we go back?' Jenny asked over her shoulder, then focussed back at the bank statements in front of her. Every month, the same three separate one thousand dollar deposits arrived into Franny's account. There was no reference number, nothing to identify the source.

'Maybe it's her pay?' Philips continued to highlight deposits.

'Marj said she was a freelance travel journalist so they could be, but all the exact same amount and every month?'

'Yeah. It doesn't seem random enough. Maybe a retainer of some sort?'

'The bank can't go back any further. Apparently, a system change means they'll need to access their archives and they charge for it, so we can't organise it unless we need the documents for a court case.'

'But without the documents, we don't know if we have a court case.' Jenny barely managed not to pout.

'I can organise a warrant, if we can find due cause. But right now, we don't have one.' O'Connell returned to his seat, adjusted his glasses and continued his own search, waiting for the adoption details to arrive.

'These entries look like cash deposits. Branch assisted, not EFT.' Jenny pointed to the reference details. 'See, they don't say online, they don't have a reference number like online transactions do.'

'Can we request information about these deposits Sir?' Philips placed the statement down on O'Connell's desk. He scanned the paperwork and nodded.

'You can make the call Philips.' He grinned, went to the main office phone and dialled the bank.

'Ask for more recent statements while you are at it.' Jenny looked to O'Connell who nodded.

'You think whoever was paying her, might not know she's dead?'

'I'm thinking, if someone killed her, they might have stopped paying her.'

Philips watched the exchange, waiting. 'Sir?'

'You can't get them over the phone. I'll request a warrant for the past few weeks.'

'I'll just ask about these then.' Philips started dialling.

'I've got that adoption report.' Jenny hurried over to O'Connell's desk and leant over his shoulder as the email downloaded the birth certificate and adoption records for Franny Kovac's baby.

'I knew it!' Jenny couldn't contain herself. 'Can I bring them in for questioning now?'

# Chapter 35

O'Connell rubbed his chin, his face contorted as he considered her question. The Senior Constable glanced up, over Jenny's shoulder. When his eyes didn't return to hers, she turned to look over her shoulder. Sergeant Mackenzie entered the office, supporting Marj, a crutch propped under her good arm.

'Look who I found hobbling her way over here.'

Jenny rushed to help. 'Marj. What's up? What have you done?'

She chuckled quietly. 'Turns out I cracked a few tiny little bones in my foot in the accident.' She stopped hobbling and held her thumb and forefinger up with a small gap. 'Didn't notice it until I did that shift in the kitchen. All that time on my feet and the bloody thing blew up like a balloon.'

'Why are you trundling across the road then?' Jenny didn't know where to touch the woman to help her. Sarge seemed content to stay at her right side and give assistance.

'I got a call, from Selene Papadakis.' Marj scrutinised Jenny with the scrunch of her nose. 'I saw you drive back with Philips and I wanted to catch you.'

Jenny glanced from Sarge, then back to Marj. 'What did Mrs Papadakis have to say?'

'You've been asking questions. Questions I should have already answered for you but didn't.' Marj's face was pale.

'Come in, take a seat.' Jenny led Marj through the open countertop and into the main office.

'Do you need to put me back in that interview room?' she grinned cheekily.

'Only if you think I should be arresting you.' Jenny's stomach knotted. Although Marj was acting buoyant, she got the distinct impression that what the motel owner was about to say might not be good news.

'Well I hope not. I watch those shows and I know technically, I could have been interfering in a police investigation and what's that other one. Yes. That's it. Obstruction of justice.'

Sarge pointed to his office. 'Let's find a seat in there. Hey?'

'Sounds good Mac. I don't think my feet will be doing any dancing in my high-heels anytime soon.'

Visions of Marj dressed in sequins, doing a Liza Minelli impression on her birthday popped into Jenny's head. The lady was a whirlwind.

Sarge pulled out his spare chair and made Marj comfortable. 'Now what's up Marj?' He rolled his office chair around his wide desk and sat beside her.

'I'm sorry luv.' She glanced up at Jenny who sat on the corner of the desk.

'About what Marj?'

'I told a little porky when I said I didn't recognise the earring. I thought it wouldn't matter. I didn't want you barking up the wrong tree or anything so I kept it to myself.'

'You know whose earring it is?' She nodded.

'You said Mrs Papadakis called you. Is it hers?'

'No luv. It's Tina's.' Jenny recalled the intricately patterned pendant design.

'Of course. I saw her necklace today. It's the same pattern. From the same set.'

Marj nodded again. 'Yes. Selene said you might have noticed it. She also said you were asking if Tina knew about the adoption.'

'We received confirmation a few minutes ago. Tina *is* Franny's biological daughter. You knew? You said you didn't know who adopted her.' Jenny's voice rose a pitch. Her stomach was tumbling with butterflies. Why had Marj lied? Were her instincts out of whack?

'Sorry. Make that two porky pies.' The slang term for lies took the edge from Jenny's anger. 'Franny told Tina she was her daughter, back when Jason died, but Con doesn't know Tina knows. So…'

'You didn't want us to push him or Tina and find out during an interview?'

'Exactly. Jason was her godfather because he was Franny's brother and he organised the adoption. Con and Jason were never close. They were on the Business Association together, so was Franny before she left town and travelled for work.'

Jenny glanced at her boss. He gave her a quick nod to continue taking the lead. 'Why was Tina's earring left in your office the night of Franny's murder?'

Marj studied her hands a moment, then glanced up, her eyes glistening with moisture. 'Franny came back to town. She was always a whirlwind that woman, but she was selfish too. She said Tina was eighteen, old enough to know the truth. She said she *needed* to know the truth.'

Jenny leant forward and squeezed Marj's hand, but something in the way she said *needed* made Jenny's skin tingle.

'*Needed*? Was that Franny's word? Did she say it like that?'

Marj rubbed her forehead, her brow creased. 'I guess she must have, but Tina and Franny fought about the adoption. She was in tears when she left Franny going through records in the back of the office.'

'Franny was in your office?' Marj nodded. 'But why, it wasn't finished?'

'We've got a back door that goes through the storeroom between the reception area and my unit.'

'What was she looking for?'

'She didn't say, but she was alive and well when Tina left her there.'

'We'll still need to hear Tina's side of the story, but if what you say is true, why didn't you come forward and tell us right away?' Sarge's tone was calmer than Jenny would have expected considering how important the information was.

*What was Franny looking for in the office?*

'Because I didn't want Con to find out Tina knew the truth. I have a feeling Franny didn't only tell Tina she was her mother. I believe she told her who her father was too.'

'Do you know who the father is?'

'No. I swear it on Jason's grave. I don't know. Franny slept with married men, single men, men with money and men with power. She knew how to keep her affairs under wraps.'

Jenny was about to ask more questions, but her mind suddenly focussed on something Marj said earlier.

'You said Jason *and* Franny were members of the Business Association, right?' A thought rolled around in her head.

'I know that look Williams. What is it?'

'I've been trying to find a link between…' She didn't want to say who in front of Marj. 'A suspect or suspects and Franny.' She pushed off the corner of the desk, grabbed Marj's face in her hands and kissed the woman's forehead. 'I think Marj just told me.'

She strode from Sarge's office without a backward glance. The last thing she heard was Marj's confused voice. 'What did I say?'

# Chapter 36

Philips had the phone to his ear, his leg jiggling as he leaned against the counter. O'Connell was stacking up the files they were working on and locking them away for the day.

'We need to interview Alexi, Con and Dragan,' she announced as O'Connell peered up from his paperwork.

'Not today Williams. We are done.'

'But Sir. I think I've worked out the link between Franny and why the Mayor's truck was outside the motel the night she died.'

Jenny caught a glimpse of Marj leaving Sarge's office. The look in her eyes revealed she overheard Jenny's comment.

'The Wednesday night, before Franny disappeared was the Business Association monthly meeting.'

'So all the members were there?' Jenny stepped toward Marj. O'Connell carried on preparing to leave.

'I don't remember for sure. I could check the minutes.'

'Where was the meeting held?'

'At the motel.'

'That could explain the F-250 being parked up the road. 'Who was the Association secretary back then?'

Jenny knew the inner workings of committees from her school days, when her mum was active in the school Parents and Friends committee. Many bored afternoons were spent watching the pedantic, methodical processes that went into minutes and motions and bla, bla, bla of committee meetings.

'Me. Well Jason used to. He was the Secretary. But they'll be in the back of the office, in a box, not sure if they got damaged in the crash.'

'Damn.'

'Tomorrow Williams.' Sarge repeated O'Connell's earlier instructions.

'Okay. Okay.' She stomped to her locker. 'I'm going home.'

Marj continued her limp past as Jenny's mobile phone pinged. She pulled it from her pocket and smiled at Nick's message. 'Hold up Marj. I'll give you a hand back to the motel. Nick's meeting me there later tonight.'

The motel owner wore bright red lipstick, to match her recent red highlights. Her eyes twinkled with mischief. 'So nice to see you two getting some *alone* time.'

Jenny blushed. Philips coughed, while Sarge and O'Connell exchanged knowing looks.

'We are just good friends Marj.'

Her vision swam with a very public kiss they shared after her last big case nearly ended badly. Who was she kidding? The cat was already well and truly out of the bag and gossip was Marj's favourite pastime.

'Sure you are.' Jenny lifted her backpack out of the locker and closed it, joining Marj in three long strides. 'I hear things you know.'

'Yes. We know.' Jenny glanced over her shoulder, rolling her eyes at her three work colleagues' stupid grins.

'Maybe you can show me where those records are, while I wait for Nick,' she whispered into Marj's ear as she supported her good arm and assisted her out of the station.

'Maybe after the dinner service. I'm still short staffed.'

'How's the new girl going?'

'She's great. Tough little one.'

'What do you mean?' Jenny steered Marj toward her Dodge ute. 'Jump in, I'll give you a lift.'

Marj patted her hand on her arm. 'I'm good. I prefer the fresh air. It's only a short hobble.'

Jenny went to protest, seriously debating if the dusty roadside and barren landscape could be considered fresh air, but she stopped herself. Marj was an independent woman. She came to Coober Pedy to be a miner, one of a handful of females willing to tough it out. She could handle herself and make her own decisions.

'If you're sure.'

'I'm sure.' They crossed the road, Marj hobbling, Jenny slowed her pace to match until the motel reception area came into view. The debris was all cleared away now and workmen had started preparing the site for reconstruction.

'How long did Con say the rebuild would take?' Jenny scanned the interior as they passed by. The gaping hole in the front was boarded up. The side door leading from the veranda was open and she could see the reception counter was gone.

The only thing remaining inside was a blocked-up door to the rear apartment where Marj usually lived and the side walls which were still plastered, having not been damaged by the vehicle impact.

She fought the urge to stop and look for the Business Association minutes.

'Con said a few weeks.'

'Do you need some help at the bar tonight, or in the kitchen?'

'No luv. You've worked all day. Take the night off. Give Nick your undivided attention.' She winked. 'I'll organise to get his room made up. You go on inside.' She let Jenny's arm go.

'Are you sure?'

'Of course.'

Jenny checked over her shoulder three times on the way to the front of the motel restaurant. Marj went in the side door to her own unit, which was freed up again now the boards were up and the debris was cleared away.

Opening the main door, she stepped into the motel bar. The smell of beer, steak and fried food reminded her she missed lunch. Cheryl glanced up from behind the bar, a quiet smile on her lips. The shorter, busty waitress focussed back on her next customer as Kelly poured two glasses of wine to fill the previous order.

The new girl was quiet, reserved with her smiles, not at all confident. Jenny wondered why Marj employed her for bar work, which usually required a more outgoing, confident personality. But she knew Marj always had a plan. There was no doubt Kelly had a story to tell and Jenny hoped she could get to know her better. There weren't a lot of younger people in Coober Pedy.

'What can we get you Jenny?' Cheryl spoke as she reached the counter. The barmaid was one of the few people, other than Nev and Tim who called her by her first name. Being a police officer in a small town meant everyone recognised her, but very few called her anything but Constable Williams.

'I'll grab a Cooper's Ale and a packet of plain chips thanks. I'll wait for Nick before dinner. When are you off tonight?'

'Not until after nine, but Kelly and I have a break in a few minutes, before the dinner rush, if you don't mind company.'

'Sounds good.'

'You nosey little bitch.' Jenny turned around to see a short, broad man pointing his stubby finger in her direction as he stormed across the room – wild eyes staring her down.

Jenny didn't recognise him. Or did she? Something about him flashed deep in her memory.

173

'You leave Con and his family alone.' The voice was loud, drawing all eyes in their direction. Quiet murmurs erupted. She stepped back from his stampede and felt for her weapon, quickly realising it was locked away.

'Sir. I'm not sure what the issue is?' Her hands were up in front of her, palms out – a technique she learnt in self-defence classes. He kept coming. Sweat broke out on her skin as adrenalin kicked up a notch.

'You're stirring up trouble with Con's family, his business. There are a lot of jobs on the line you know.' He was nose to nose with her now, his finger poking her chest with hard, stabbing motions. Her body swayed backwards, trying to avoid the harsh finger jabs, but he kept prodding her chest.

Voices grew louder around her, but her focus was fixed on the man in front of her as sound fell away and her instincts kicked in. He thrust another finger into her chest. Her hand snapped shut, twisting it up hard. He cried out. She spun him around by his arm in one smooth motion.

His back was to her now, his arm pulled up hard behind his back. 'Do I need to arrest you for assaulting a police officer?' She leant over his shoulder, her voice forced politeness.

Two men, who had stepped forward, ready to assist her stopped, grinned and chuckled as her assailant squealed. 'Ah! Ouch! No!'

She thrusted his arm up hard behind his back. 'I'm going to let your hand go now. Okay?' He nodded. 'Then you are going to answer a few civil questions. Okay?'

He didn't answer. She gave his arm another push. He tried to reach her with his free hand, but couldn't. She pressed his arm higher again, forcing him toward the bar. Cheryl jumped away as the big man careered into the timber which rattled with the impact. Another thrust of his arm made him groan.

'Okay?'

'Yeah! Ouch! Got it.' She held his arm a moment longer, just to be sure.

'Let's start from the beginning hey.' She gently released him. He turned to face her, hands held high, like she was a gunslinger robbing a bank.

'Other than come to the yard twice to ask questions, we've done nothing to interrupt Con's business. What's *your* issue?'

The man shuffled his feet like a schoolboy in the Headmaster's office. Now that he was calm, Jenny could see his flushed cheeks and red nose.

He sniffed. 'Since you came, the family have been screaming at each other. If Mrs divorces Mr we'll lose our jobs while they fight over money.'

Jenny frowned. 'Look mate. Even if they did divorce, which I don't think they are…' not that she knew for sure, but she wanted to keep him calm, 'the business is where all the money comes from. He's not going to be closing it down to pay out his wife. Refinance maybe?'

'But Mrs P. *is* the money,' he insisted.

'What's your name?' Jenny drew him away from the bar, toward a quiet corner. He frowned but said nothing. 'I'm not pressing charges. I'm not telling anyone about this.' She scrutinised all the onlookers who were now going back to their beers. 'I can't speak for the crowd here, but I'd like to understand what makes you think Mrs Papadakis has all the money?'

'I've been with *Papas Construction* for more than ten years. A few years back, Con had cashflow problems.' Jenny's mind began to churn details over.

'How many years ago?'

'I don't know five maybe six.'

'And you think Mrs Papadakis bailed the business out?'

He scanned over his shoulder, suddenly aware that he likely made a spectacle right in the middle of one of the busiest bars in town. 'The Papadakis family are passionate people. You kinda hear every little argument even from outside the office,' he whispered.

'You were eavesdropping.'

He sighed. 'Just watching out for the boys on the team.'

'And what did you hear?'

'An argument, between Con and his Missus. They were arguing about money. Mrs Papadakis' family were loaded. Old man Georgiou, that's Mrs P.'s dad, owned a huge cotton farm out on the Hay Plains. He died. Mrs P. was the sole beneficiary. Sold it for a mint.'

'Was she happy about loaning him the money?'

'I didn't hear the details. I don't know,' he pouted.

'Well, if Mrs Papadakis is loaded, why are you worried about a divorce causing you issues? If Selene Papadakis has lots of her own money, she is unlikely to need to get more out of Con in a divorce.'

'I don't know how these things work.' He scowled. 'But I don't want you stirring up any more trouble.' His fist was clenched at his side as he resisted the urge to shake his finger at her.

'I'm not stirring up trouble. I'm investigating a murder and Mr and Mrs Papadakis are helping with our enquiries.' She needed his details and a statement or all of this was just hearsay. 'You didn't tell me your name.'

'Well your enquiries got the whole family at each other's throats.'

'Tina too?'

The man nodded. 'Look, give me your name. Let me take a statement.'

'No way. I'm not giving you any more reason to shut Con down.'

'Why would I do that, unless you think he's involved in Franny Kovac's murder.'

The man turned around, scanning every face in the bar with wide eyes. 'I'm out of here. I shouldn't have said anything. One too many beers. I'm just rambling like an idiot. Forget I said anything.'

He rushed toward the door. Jenny couldn't stop him. He was over a hundred and twenty kilograms moving at full speed for the front door. As he stormed off, Cheryl rushed over.

'Are you okay?' She scanned Jenny for injuries with her hands.

'I'm fine.'

'That was amazing,' she nearly hooted. 'Can you teach me how to do that?'

Kelly rushed up alongside Cheryl. 'And me too.'

# Chapter 37

The crowd in the bar was thinning out as Nick sat down, beer in hand. 'I've got our order in before they shut the kitchen. Sorry I'm so late. Had to oversee a few last-minute things before I could leave the boys looking after the place a day early.'

'I'm so glad you made it out tonight.' Jenny shuffled her chair closer to him, trying to drown out the few late revellers.

He reached for her hand. 'You okay?'

'Yep. I'm good. Just had a bit of a run-in with one of *Papa Construction's* workers earlier though.'

'And she handled herself like a champ.' Cheryl slid in next to Nick. 'I hope I'm not interrupting?'

Jenny grinned up at Cheryl as Nick pulled out the chair on the other side from Jenny.

'No. You're fine.' He sipped his beer, locking eyes with Jenny as Cheryl shuffled into the seat. 'Are you finding trouble again?' He lifted an eyebrow in question.

'No.' She lifted her chin. 'Trouble is finding me.'

Nick's tone was calm, but his eyes were worried. 'You get that a lot.'

'Jenny grabbed his arm, twisted him around like he was a ragdoll. You should have seen it Nick.' Cheryl's hands were flying in every direction. A rare Nick Johnston smile broke out. 'She's going to teach me and Kelly how to do that. Next jerk who grabs my arse is going to regret it.'

'There's a code to go with it Cheryl. You can't hurt every guy you don't like.' Jenny drank the last of her beer. 'Self-defence is just that. It's not an offensive action.' Her martial arts instructor's lectures popped into her mind.

'I get it.' Her eyes were wide with excitement.

'Besides, if you break the arm of every guy who grabs your butt, Marj will have no patrons left.' Cheryl laughed.

Nick frowned. 'That's sad. Do you get groped that often?'

Cheryl rolled her eyes. 'When I'm behind the counter, I'm safe, but not out in the main bar area. Nearly every night, at least a half dozen times, something happens. Sometimes it's subtle, like a brush of the crotch against my hip and a fake *Oh, sorry about that Sweetheart.* But other times, just a good old-fashioned squeeze.

'That's shocking.' Nick didn't hide his outrage.

Cheryl shrugged. 'I have a reputation. I guess that does encourage more than the average grab. Jenny here doesn't have such a big issue I'm guessing.'

'I think the uniform helps.' She tugged her collar.

'No. You aren't known as the local slut like I am.' Cheryl tried to look tough, but failed.

When Jenny came to town, Cheryl's best friend Tiffany was found murdered. During the investigation, Jenny discovered both women had turned favours in exchange for accommodation and a little money.

Even Nick had been tough on Tiffany at one point, when she tried to cosy up with his little brother Sam, but she was young, vulnerable and virtually homeless with few choices. It infuriated Jenny to know that someone took advantage of the girls when they were young and now it was the mature women paying the price.

'I've told you before Cheryl. You're worth more than you think.'

'Jenny's right. The right guy will come around.'

The order buzzer vibrated on the table. Nick stood. 'I'll get it. Do you want another beer?'

'No. I want to go over some paperwork later, in Marj's office, if you don't mind.' She shrugged apologetically. Nick's lips turned up in a slight grin.

'Always on the job Constable.'

'Sorry. I just want my caseload clear so I can work on other things.' Nick nodded, knowing what *other things* she was referring to. He turned and strolled, vibrating buzzer in hand to collect their meals.

'He's a keeper you know.' Cheryl squeezed her hand on the table.

'I know.' She glanced up to see Kelly passing the meals over to Nick. 'What's her story?'

'I don't know much. She lived with a commune of some sort, on the outskirts of town. Cult if you ask me. But she seems okay now. Maybe when you teach us Karate, we can find out more.'

'Self-defence.' Jenny corrected.

'Self-defence.' Cheryl saluted. 'I've got to help with clean up. See you later.'

Cheryl rushed past as Nick put the food down on the table and pulled out his chair to slide in. 'I missed you.' He lifted her fingers to his lips, the sensation making her tummy tingle.

'I missed you too.' She knew she was blushing, so averted her eyes. Something drew her focus. She frowned. Nick turned to see what she could see.

'What's up?'

'I don't know,' she shuddered. 'I felt like someone was watching me.'

'Well you are pretty beautiful you know.'

'Oh stop it.' She gently slapped his shoulder. The warmth of his hand on hers, the closeness of his body, the smell of his aftershave, all made her pulse quicken.

Visions of Nick's motel room filled her mind. She shook her head. She wasn't ready. Was she? Thoughts of the Business Association minutes and cold cases disappeared to the recesses of her consciousness as Nick leant forward to brush his lips on hers.

'You are you know. I can see you don't believe it, but Jenny Williams, you are a gorgeous lady.'

She blushed again. 'You're pretty hot yourself.'

# Chapter 38

Marj sat on a chair, her single crutch leant against a beaten-up filing cabinet. Nick reached up to retrieve a brown and tan striped filing box labelled B.A. on the front in black marker pen.

'I think that is the last one. They must be in there.' Marj's eyes were pinched.

'Your leg hurting? Or is it your arm?' Jenny put her hand on the older woman's shoulder.

'Both. A little, but I'm fine. Nothing a shot of brandy won't cure.' Her chuckle was deep. Her smile genuine.

'Okay.' Nick dropped the box on the desk inside Marj's back-office area. Although untouched by the crash, dust had settled on everything in the room.

'Let's see what we can find.' Jenny struggled to remove the tightly fitted lid. Nick helped pry the edges up.

Once open, Jenny reached inside to retrieve a wad of A4 papers. Handing Marj a chunk from the top, then another slab for Nick, she grabbed the rest for herself. Sitting down at the desk, she started scanning minutes.

'You said you wanted the minutes from June twenty ten, right?' Nick shuffled papers.

'It might be worth checking out a few months before and after.'

'I won't have after.' Marj was busy scanning loose pieces of paperwork.

'Why not?'

'Because I only filled in while Jason was sick. Once he passed, I told them to elect a new secretary. I was done with it anyway.'

'Any particular reason?'

'They are an incestuous bunch.'

Nick laughed. 'I don't think you mean that literally Marj.'

'I wouldn't be so sure.' Marj waved a piece of paper as she spoke.

'Do you want to explain?' Jenny scrutinised her, coaxing for more.

'I don't know how Jason put up with them. Always talking about who was going to make sure who got the next big government contract and of course, when Alexi became Mayor, it only got worse.'

'That maybe corruption Marj, but incestuous means something totally different.' Jenny was fairly sure Marj knew the meaning of the word. She wasn't some pretty, naïve schoolgirl.

'Con wants Tina to marry Alexi. It doesn't get more incestuous than that!' she scoffed.

Jenny stopped looking at paperwork and fixed her gaze on Marj. 'What do you mean?'

Marj bit her lip. 'It's only a rumour.' She shuffled papers vigorously. 'Let's just find these minutes. Ah, here they are.' She waved two pieces of paper stapled together in the air.

'Marj!'

'Alexi, Con, Dragan and Franny were all there.' She kept her eyes on the paperwork, ignoring Jenny's harsh stare.

Jenny rubbed her temples, trying to suppress the imminent headache that came with trying to make sense of what Marj was saying.

'Okay.' She let the incest comment go. 'Why was Franny at the meeting? I thought she was only in town for Jason's Will reading?'

'I forgot she stood in for me. I was a right mess as you can imagine.'

'So our victim, was with at least two of our suspects the night she died?' Jenny tossed the papers in her hand down hard on the desk. Dust rose into the dimly lit room. Marj gaped at her.

'And what did you mean by incest if Tina marries Alexi?' She put her hands on her hips and rounded on Marj. 'You're still keeping something under your hat. I can feel it in my gut. You're usually all speculation in these cases. Come on. Spill it.'

Marj shuffled the papers in her hands, ignoring Jenny. 'Don't you want to know who else was at the meeting?'

'In a minute.' She stepped forward, looming over Marj. Nick cleared his throat. She turned to see his eyes focussed on hers, trying to tell her something. Her stomach rolled as she realised she was interrogating one of her closest friends.

She pulled back. Marj's face wore a mix of emotions. Shame, guilt, frustration.

'I'm sorry Marj.'

She sighed. 'It's okay luv. I get it. I want to see Franny's murderer punished too, but some secrets aren't supposed to be spoken out loud.'

Jenny thought about her cousin. About her leaving town and running away and how everyone in her family seemed to be a closed book about it. She shook her head. There were no good secrets. Secrets were dangerous, scary and painful.

'If you knew who Tina's father was, you'd tell me. Right?'

'If I knew, but I don't.' She shut her mouth and shook her head like a petulant child.

********

Ten minutes later, Jenny was compiling the minutes from the meeting for the night Franny died and the three months prior. Her limbs were heavy, but her heart weighed a ton when she considered nearly losing her cool with Marj.

'I shouldn't have pushed her.'

'You do get carried away sometimes.' Nick wrapped his arm around her shoulder as they stepped from the office area, leaving Marj to lock up and go to bed. 'Come on. You've got what you came for. Time to go.' He gently steered her down onto the veranda.

His room was one way, her car the other. She hesitated. 'I have an early start.'

Nick wrapped his other arm around her, gently moving her back to the brick wall and holding her gaze. 'This is new Jenny. I'm not in any rush.'

'But Nick I...' He touched his finger to her lips to silence her before gently lowering his lips to hers. The kiss was feather light. Her whole body quivered.

'I'm glad we could catch up.' His voice was husky.

'Are you sure?' She whispered, not certain if she was happy he was okay with waiting.

'I'll walk you to your car.' He grasped her hands in his and gently pulled her away from the wall. Keeping a hold of one hand, he guided her from the motel and across the front carpark.

'Thanks.' Her words sounded hollow to her own ears.

Nick pulled her close, sensing her thoughts as they strolled toward the police station and her car. The street was dark except for the crescent moon and stars shining above. The aromatic scent of eucalyptus lingered on the still night air as they stepped toward the station porch light – their only indication they were heading in the right direction, but Jenny knew the way by heart now.

She hugged the paperwork to her chest with one arm. 'I can't wait to see how the homestead rebuild is going. I hope I can make it out soon.'

'It would be good to show you around, but there's still nowhere for you to stay.'

'I can probably manage the sheering quarters.'

'I'm sure you could, but I'm not sure they can manage you.'

Jenny was about to ask what he meant when a sound made her stop and scan her surroundings. The sensation of being watched was back.

'What's that?' Nick scanned the vacant street with her. No cars, no people, no lights, no anything. It was after ten and this time of year, nothing happened late at night.

A revving motor made Jenny's skin tingle. Every hair on her head jumped to attention as her body stiffened.

'Get moving!' Nick shoved her toward her parked car. She ran as the sound of tyres spinning on gravel made her heart skip a beat.

A few steps from her car, she tripped. Scanning past Nick, she heard the sound draw closer, but still there were no lights. Nick dragged her to her feet, physically lifting her with brute strength.

'Get to your car.' Nick's voice sounded panicked. He never panicked. He was always so cool. So calm.

Jenny's feet moved like they were weighed down with rocks. Her mind saw where she wanted to go, but her body wasn't getting there fast enough. As she slid around the front end of her Dodge, Nick close behind, every fibre of her body was rigid with tension.

A dark coloured ute with loud growling tyres sped toward them. Jenny ducked down. The vehicle collided with the right-side door and front end of her truck, propelling it hard into them. Nick flung himself at Jenny, dragging her to the ground with him as gravel and dust filled the air around them.

Jenny strained to get a glimpse of the rear of the vehicle and the number plate, but the rear light over the number plate was broken. In the dark, it was impossible to make out the vehicle model and colour.

'Are you alright?' Nick was short of breath. His eyes scanned her in the moonlight. Standing, he gently pulled her to her feet.

'I think so. You?' Her body shook with adrenalin.

'I'm good.' He pulled her close, hugging her to his chest. She could feel his heart pounding as much as hers. 'What was that all about?' he whispered.

Jenny turned her head to stare along the empty road. There was no point trying to chase them. They were gone. 'It could be the guy who bailed me up in the bar tonight, or maybe we've rattled Franny's killer?'

Nick held her at arm's length. His face impossible to read in the darkness. 'Or it could be about dad's murder, maybe?'

He was right. Was she the target, or was Nick? 'Maybe it was just a drunken idiot on their way home from the bar.'

'And they forgot to put their lights on?'

'It's been known to happen.' Jenny could hear her own voice, it wasn't convincing anyone. Nick drew her back into a firm embrace which she was thankful for. The night suddenly felt colder than it was.

# Chapter 39

The team hovered around the whiteboard in the main office area as O'Connell dropped the desk phone handset into the cradle with a thud.

'BOLO is out.'

'I didn't see much. It was a regular looking dark coloured utility with big growling tyres, but it will have a nice gash in the front left quarter where it hit my poor old Dodge.'

'It could be unrelated to the case. Some drunk leaving the motel without putting his lights on.' Jenny thought about Philips' comment – she said the same to Nick, but when Jenny replayed the scene in her mind, there was no doubt the car swerved towards them as they casually strolled across the road.

'I did have one of Con's workers have a go at me in the bar last night. I thought I calmed him down, but maybe not. Don't know his name though.'

'What did he say?' Sarge shifted papers to find space to sit on the edge of O'Connell's desk.

'He told me to stop hassling the Papadakis family because they were all fighting since we first visited.'

'Interesting.' Sarge dragged his hand over his mouth and chin, then tapped his nose with his finger.

A murder and subsequent investigation created mistrust, and often tore a rift in a small community like Coober Pedy. Local policing was tough enough, without being the bad guy hassling locals for answers.

'I thought so. He also said Con's business needed bailing out back around the time Franny died and that Selene loaned him the money from her inheritance.'

'Why would he tell you that?'

'Because he was worried Selene was divorcing Con over Franny's murder investigation and he blamed me. Told me I would send the business broke.'

'That's a good reason to try to run you over.' Sarge pushed off the desk to leave. 'I'll go see Marj's team and see if anyone recognised him. Let's get into this people. It was a cold case yesterday, but not today. Today, it's connected to a near miss of one of our own.'

He stopped on his way through the counter, turned, his hand resting on top. 'Seems your reputation is growing Williams.' He grinned, then his features grew serious. 'Just watch your back.' He turned and left.

Jenny glanced at O'Connell. He was watching Sarge leave, his expression worried.

'Everything okay Sir?' She spoke quietly, so Philips couldn't hear.

'He's getting attached to you Williams.'

She shrugged, unsure why that was an issue. It certainly made her life a lot easier. O'Connell could see she didn't understand the issue.

'You won't be here forever.' O'Connell's eyes darted down to his screen, his fingers tapped keys as Philips handed her a wad of paperwork.

'The last month of Franny Kovac's bank records. Not much here, other than deposits.' He waved at a small pile in his own hand.

'I'd hope not, or someone has been accessing a dead woman's bank account.' She collected the sheets from Philips and browsed through. 'Those three deposits are still coming in.'

'What on earth for?' O'Connell's whole face creased with confusion.

'We need to find out where these deposits are coming from and what they are payment for.' Jenny gave the paperwork back to Philips.

'You'll need to go directly to the bank.' O'Connell tapped keys on his keyboard. 'I've sent a copy of the warrant to your email. Follow it up Philips.'

'Will do Sir.'

'Another thing Sir.' O'Connell gave Jenny his attention. 'Marj alluded to Tina's father possibly being Alexi Samaras last night. I find that disturbing.'

'That might explain why he's popped up for interviews with Con and been putting the pressure on to stop questioning the locals about Franny.'

'Surely if he knew he was Tina's father, he wouldn't be trying to marry her?'

'We know Franny had a reputation. Almost anyone could be Tina's father, but Alexi putting on the pressure does raise suspicion.' O'Connell wrestled with his glasses as he peered over the top, trying to focus from his computer screen to Jenny.

'We have her DNA. We could run it.' Jenny brought the subject up knowing it would likely go nowhere. 'I sent it to the lab, just in case.'

'I told you we won't get that back for months. Only urgent cases get priority. For now, keep digging, get details of who is making those bank deposits. We need to leave Tina and her family alone for now.'

'Okay, but whoever it is, can't be Franny's murderer, or they would have stopped paying.'

'Or they kept paying so they would look innocent.' O'Connell's eyes returned to his computer, the conversation over.

'Okay. Let's get to work.' Jenny joined Philips at the counter computer. 'Find anything yet?'

'I need to get the local branch to send over video footage from the cameras for the past month. Check the time and date of these deposits and then go through the footage.'

Jenny tapped his shoulder. 'Good luck with that.' She grinned. He rolled his eyes.

Sorting through the highlighted phone records, she studied the numbers. All but Tom Hammond contacted Franny in the twenty-four hours before Wednesday night, but there were multiple calls back and forth between the one number.

'Forensics have uncovered some hair that doesn't match the colour or consistency of the victim's.' O'Connell tapped more keys as he spoke. 'No DNA though. Too old and no hair follicles were found.'

'Any idea what the original colour would have been? Or anything else of interest?' Jenny flicked through the paperwork.

'McGregor's report is here. Something about it being Caucasian, but unusually thick.'

Jenny was half listening, her eyes still scanning the phone records. 'I've found something Sir.' She picked up a sheet of paper and rushed to the Senior Constable's desk. 'Franny received calls from nearly everyone in our suspect pool the days before she died, but she called these three numbers the most leading up to her death.'

'I'll get a trace on them now.' O'Connell started tapping keys.

'I already checked all these numbers before I started searching the records.' O'Connell waited. 'These are Con, Alexi and Dragan's numbers.'

'So we have three men contacting Franny and three one thousand dollar deposits going into her bank account every month from a local branch?'

'Yes Sir. Coincidence or, in light of what Marj was saying last night, maybe it's hush money.'

'Three men, two married, one the local Mayor, all possibly having a relationship with Franny Kovac, but why hush money?'

'Paternity maybe?'

# Chapter 40

Sarge barged into the conversation as he returned from the motel. 'Got an ID on Con's employee.'

O'Connell pursed his lips. Jenny opened her mouth to update her Sergeant, but he carried on. 'Site supervisor, and guess what car he drives?'

'A dark coloured utility?'

'Bingo.'

'We might have something else to follow up,' O'Connell interrupted.

'More important than questioning the guy who tried to run Williams over?'

'No, but we can do both. Con, Dragan and Alexi all called Franny in the days leading up to her murder. We believe all three have been making monthly deposits into Franny's account – at least it looks that way.' O'Connell pointed to Philips. 'Put a rush on the video footage.' He returned his attention to Sarge. 'Just waiting on bank security videos, but it's looking like Franny might have been blackmailing them all over Tina's paternity.'

Sarge screwed up his face. His lips rolled inward as he considered the information.

'That's our working theory anyway.' Jenny spoke into his silence.

'Find if any crash repairers have a dark coloured utility in for body work. Get that video footage. We don't move on anything until we know what we've got.' He stomped to his office, suddenly unsatisfied with his earlier discovery.

'What's the site foreman's name?' Jenny called. He stopped outside his office door.

'Nicolas Fletcher.'

'Philips, run a search. Williams, check wreckers.' O'Connell barked orders as Sarge slammed his door.

'All three men are linked with Franny on the night of her death since they all attended the Business Association meeting. I have the minutes. Franny acted as secretary because Marj wasn't in any state.'

'Didn't Dragan say he had dinner with his wife that night?' O'Connell scribbled notes on a pad at his desk.

'He did. Maybe he had dinner after the meeting. That would put him in the clear, but it's a long time ago. The only person corroborating that will be his wife.'

O'Connell pursed his lip at her comment, tapped his pen and continued writing notes. 'Williams, what time did Marj say Tina argued with Franny? Was that the last time she was seen alive?'

'I'll check my notes Sir.' She had a sneaking suspicion she didn't note the time. What a rookie error. She'd need to ask Marj.

'Philips, run vehicle details for Fletcher, and our other three suspects.'

'On it now Sir, but we know Dragan has Alexi's F-250.' Philips typed details into his computer while Jenny shuffled the paperwork into a pile.

'We need to interview all three of them.' Jenny frowned at Sergeant Mackenzie's closed door. 'He's not going to like this.'

'Sarge is right. We need to have all the evidence stockpiled first, but leave him to me.' O'Connell glanced at the door, stood up from his desk and crossed the room to stand behind Philips. 'Any hit on the car?'

Philips pointed to his screen. Jenny couldn't see past O'Connell. 'That's interesting.' O'Connell stepped away and strode toward Sarge's door.

'What?' Jenny stepped up to the computer. Philips pointed. 'Con's car?'

'I didn't see it at the yard the other day.' Philips printed out the ownership details.

'Me neither. Maybe it's part of his work fleet.' Jenny thought about the disgruntled employee who bailed her up in the Motel bar. 'It still could be Fletcher.'

'Maybe we should pay him a visit?'

'We'll bring Con in first.' Sarge appeared outside his office, flanked by O'Connell.

'What about the Mayor?' Jenny knew the answer before she asked it, but it was worth a shot.

'We've got nothing on him yet. Con's connected to the vehicle. To Tina. To Franny. We'll start there.' Sarge didn't look happy, but with so much evidence stacking up, he didn't have a choice.

'You two go get Con. I'll see if I can get the bank video any quicker.' O'Connell crossed to his desk as Jenny reached into her locker, retrieving her utility vest and taser.

Signing for her service weapon, she turned to find Philips right behind her.

'Ready?' he asked as he checked his pistol and placed it into his waist holster.

'Ready.'

# Chapter 41

It was 10 a.m. on a Friday, too early for the construction company yard to be closed, but that's exactly what they found when they pulled up outside *Papas Construction's* front mesh fence. A large padlock held the double gates closed.

Beyond, silence greeted them. The office door was closed. No vehicles were parked in the front yard. The concrete plant was still.

'What's going on?' Jenny turned in a slow circle, trying to work out where to look next.

Philips glanced at his watch for the third time. 'It's not a public holiday.' He scratched the back of his head.

'Maybe Con was driving the ute that nearly hit me and Nick last night?'

'We'll call past his house.'

'Where's that?'

'His place is out on Gem Place. You wanted to see a fancy dugout, their place definitely fits the bill.'

'I didn't see Selene living in a dugout.'

'They did this place up years ago. Before I was born.'

'How do you know about it then?'

'Mum and dad used to talk about it all the time. Mum wanted to do a fixer-upper herself, but dad wasn't interested.'

Philips guided the Police Landcruiser through back streets Jenny was unfamiliar with. Homes of all shapes lined the roads. Many were refurbished dugouts. A few were brand new builds which looked out of place against the sparse red and sandstone landscape.

'A fixer. Makes sense since Con is a builder I guess. And Fletcher told me Mrs Papadakis has a load of money.'

'They were dead broke back then. You said Mrs Papadakis got her money after her dad died. That's long after they did this place up and Con's business took off. From what mum says, it was mostly Selene who did the work on it because Con was flat chat trying to build up their business.'

'Good on her. Nothing wrong with a handy woman.'

The four-wheel drive jostled as they navigated the long, rough driveway.

'Looks like the track needs some maintenance.'

'Let's hope Con is home.' Jenny slammed the door, checked her weapon was secure and joined Philips as they strolled toward the front door.

Scanning the area, Jenny kept her eyes open for the dark coloured ute but the front yard was vacant of any vehicles. Maybe there was a shed around the back, but that seemed unlikely. The dugout was built into a rounded mound of solid rock.

An ochre and sandstone stone wall loomed above a metal bullnose veranda which spanned the full length. Small, colonial style windows faced out from under the veranda, built into a weatherboard clad wall.

Jenny peered over her shoulder as Philips rang the doorbell.

A muted chime sounded within. Jenny and Philips hung back, waiting for the door to open. A few minutes passed and Jenny was about to press the buzzer again when a slide-lock sounded and the door handle wiggled.

Tina peered out, her gaze jumping from Jenny to Philips as a deep crease almost joined her thick eyebrows in the middle of her forehead.

'Tina. Is Con home?'

'Dad!' She called over her shoulder. 'Come in.' She lowered her voice and stepped back.

Jenny entered the foyer, Philips directly behind her. In front of her a tunnel disappeared like a long hallway. The thick sandstone walls featured wall lights which illuminated deep circular marks from the drilling machine left behind after years of unearthing opals. To her left and right, short plaster walls framed two wide case openings leading to a living and dining area on her left, while the kitchen and smaller eat-in area was on the right.

'I've been desperate to see a fancy dugout. This place is awesome.' Jenny knew she was gawking, but couldn't help herself.

'What's up?' Tina asked as she showed them through the left opening into the living area.

'We need to speak with your dad.'

'I'll go get him.' Tina disappeared down the long stone hallway.

Jenny wandered around perusing the walls, observing the photos of the family when Tina was younger. Selene Papadakis was nearly as tall as Con, which wasn't very tall. Her face glowed as she held a baby in her arms. More photos showed the transformation of the old opal mine into a family home.

A collage of photos caught her eye. Selene covered in paint, in old overalls, working on the plaster walls in the foyer.

'What do you need Officers?'

'Mr Papadakis.' Jenny left the photos and joined Philips to meet Con. 'The office is closed today. Is everything alright?'

'Selene is sick in bed. This week has been,' he rubbed his chin, 'difficult on her'.

'I'm sorry to hear that.' Jenny glanced at Philips. His face showed his sympathy. 'Unfortunately, we need to bring you down the station for some questions Con.'

'Dad. What's going on?' Tina grasped his arm.

'It's fine Tina. It's only a few questions. Look after your mum. I'll be back soon.' He gently removed her hand.

The behaviour seemed the total opposite of what they witnessed in the office the other day. Con's tone was calm. Maybe he and Mrs Papadakis were one of those couples who knew exactly how to set each other off in an argument.

'Thanks for coming along sir.' Philips opened the front door.

'What's this about?' Con followed Philips out the door, Jenny turned to glance at Tina, but before she could pull the door shut, she saw the younger woman speed off down the narrow hallway. No doubt to tell her mum what was going on.

'You own a black Mitsubishi four-wheel drive utility. Is it here?'

'I own three. They are all work cars.'

Jenny opened the rear passenger's side door. 'Are they here? I didn't see any at the yard.'

Con frowned at the open door. 'I can drive myself.'

'We'd rather you accompany us.'

'Am I under arrest? Do I need a lawyer?' His gaze jumped from her to Philips and back.

'You're not under arrest, but you are welcome to call a lawyer if you feel you need one.' Jenny ushered him into the backseat with a wave. The tone of her voice told him that calling a lawyer now would only fuel their suspicion.

'My vehicles are spread out. One is in the shed at work. I don't drive a ute. I have a Lexus SUV I prefer.'

'Where are the other two?'

'One is with my foreman, Nicolas Fletcher.'

'I've met Nicolas.' Jenny put her seatbelt on, catching Philips' grin out the corner of her eye. He glanced in the rear-view mirror as he started the engine.

'And the other one?' Philips asked as he backed out of the parking spot and turned the vehicle to head down the bumpy driveway once more.

'I don't know.'

Jenny turned. 'You don't know, or you don't want to say?'

# Chapter 42

The interview room was cramped, but Jenny was sure those in the know designed them that way to be more intimidating.

Con sat opposite her. O'Connell led the interview. At first, she was put out by being pulled back from leading the interview, but Sarge assured her it had nothing to do with her and more to do with Con's position in the small mining town.

She observed O'Connell's method. Other than his recent outburst with the lead singer of a country rock band who wasn't cooperating with their inquiries, O'Connell had always remained calm and quiet during interviews.

Today was no different. The Senior Constable sat back, looking more casual than he should.

'Con.'

'John.'

'Not looking good mate.'

'What's going on?'

'One of your company utes tried to run down our overzealous Constable and her boyfriend last night.'

Jenny lifted her eyebrows at the reference to Nick and her zeal, but said nothing.

'Nothing to do with me and what makes you think it was one of my vehicles?'

'We have a very reliable witness.' O'Connell's smile failed to reach his eyes.

Other than recently discovering O'Connell was formerly married to the newspaper owner, Jenny was struck by how little she knew about him. There was an untold story there she was dying to uncover.

'I fail to see how a road incident I wasn't involved in could put me in a poor light.'

O'Connell tutted. 'Just got word that some money was going into Franny's account, at the local branch, every month mate. Won't take much to prove you were depositing it.'

Con put his elbows on the interview desk, his head fell into his hands as his chest rose with slow, ragged breaths.

Finally, he looked up, his eye meeting O'Connell's, pupils enlarged, iris's glistening with unshed tears. 'I didn't kill Franny.'

'She was Tina's mother. Who's her father?' O'Connell's question made Con's eyes open wide. O'Connell's tone was firm; the question so direct it caught the man off guard.

Con opened his mouth, closed it, drew a quick breath through his nose, then rolled his lips together. He was going to clam up. Jenny's instincts were screaming at her. He was going to call for a lawyer, any second. She opened her mouth to say something, but O'Connell's sharp glance her way stopped her.

'She's supposed to have married Alexi years ago.' The change of subject seemed out of place. Con didn't exactly relax, but her fear he was ready to lawyer up abated. This was about his family and all the photos on his walls told her family was important to him or at least to Selene.

Con shrugged. Jenny recalled the argument in the yard office. From her observation, it appeared to be about the impending marriage. Selene said as much, but something about the scene struck her as strange and Con's nonchalant attitude now bugged her.

A knot sat in her chest as she forced down the urge to interrupt the interview with a question. She needed to let O'Connell finish. He was a seasoned officer. She needed to learn to trust her team and let go of her urge to control everything.

'Why is that Con?' O'Connell's tone was casual.

'She's not ready.' Con fidgeted.

*She's in love with someone else.* Jenny kept the thought to herself.

'Is Alexi her father?' Jenny opened her mouth, then closed it. 'Tina knows she's adopted now, right?' O'Connell knew according to Marj, Franny told Tina the truth. It was hearsay, a stab in the dark though, without confirmation from Tina.

But the bombshell was dropped and out in the open now. Tina could be Alexi's daughter. Surely Con would know if she was. She shuddered at the thought of Tina being forced to marry her own father.

Con's eyes grew round, then narrowed. He spluttered. Sounds came out of his mouth but nothing coherent.

'I think we have enough for a warrant. Money going into Franny's account.' He glanced at Jenny. She nodded seriously, her poker face back in place. Con looked from her to O'Connell, then licked his lips. 'A DNA test should do the trick.'

'You can't.' Con pleaded.

'Why not?' Still that calm, casual tone.

Jenny was impressed. Con didn't seem surprised Tina's father could be Alexi, but he desperately didn't want Tina to know. Why? Was he paying Franny to keep quiet? Maybe he was embarrassed he betrothed Tina to her own father? Or... maybe Con knew he was the father not Alexi and didn't want his wife to find out?

A prolonged, scraping sound like chalk on a blackboard made Jenny shiver as Con slowly slid his chair back along the worn lino floor, rose and leant over the interview desk. His eyes drilled into O'Connell's.

'I think we are done unless you have charges you want to lay.'

'You're not leaving without the location of all three Mitsubishi Utilities registered to the company Con.'

His cheeks puffed out. 'I told you, one is locked in the yard. One is with Nicolas.'

'And the third?' O'Connell waited. Con sighed.

'Is getting some work done on it.'

'Work?' O'Connell pointed to the seat. Con sat back down.

'Selene bumped into a rubbish bin.'

'I'll get Philips to contact the panel beaters to tell them to stop work on it.' Jenny tried not to rush as she rose from her seat.

'Constable Williams is leaving the interview.' O'Connell spoke for the recording. 'You better hope Selene has witnesses to that bin incident mate.'

# Chapter 43

Jenny's head was spinning. Why would Selene try to run her over? Maybe she didn't. Maybe Con was using her as an excuse.

Alexi or Con were involved with Franny, but they needed to trace the money to be sure.

'I need to check with the crash repairers. Con said Selene had a run in with a rubbish bin in one of the three black utes in his fleet. We need to stop any repairs so we can see if it is the vehicle that struck my car.'

'On it. There are only two in town. I hadn't had a chance to ring either yet. It's been like a bus station in here.' Philips opened a browser and typed in the details of the first. 'You call this one. I'll call the other.' He pointed to a number on the screen.

Jenny wrote the number down on a scrap of paper and rushed over to the shared work desk. She still needed to interview Tina about the argument she had with Franny the night she died. It hadn't seemed a priority, but now one of Con's cars could be the one that tried to run her over, it made sense to push Tina a little harder.

'Blue Sky Crash, Marty speaking.'

'Hey Marty. This is Constable Williams from local police. Just chasing down a vehicle you might have in your shop for repair.'

'Ah..' There was moment of hesitation, then a chuckle. 'That's right, you're the new cop. The one with the great set of lungs.'

Jenny rolled her eyes. Her first night in town led to too many drinks with Penny and Nev and apparently she put on quite the show at the Karaoke mic, and she was still living it down.

'That's me. Do you have a black Mitsubishi ute in there with a left front and side impact?'

'Sure do. Was about to start on it for Con.'

'Don't touch it. We'll be down in fifteen minutes.'

'Ah…what's up?'

'It is a vehicle of interest in a possible unreported collision. No panic. Just don't let anyone touch it. Okay?'

'You got it Constable.' The phone line went dead. Jenny hung up as Philips did the same.

'At Blue Sky. I'll let O'Connell know and we can get going now.'

'Okay. I'll grab the keys.'

Jenny stopped by her locker, grabbed her vest and then signed out her service weapon. She was pulling the vest on over her head as she opened the interview door.

'Sir. We've located the vehicle.'

Con chewed his lip.

'Good work Williams. Looks like we are done then Con. Call your lawyer mate. You might need him.'

They made good time, getting to the crash repairers in less than ten minutes. The black utility was parked at the front of the first shed bay. An open tray with shiny roll bars was untouched, a long graze ran down the left-hand side.

The front light was broken and the door bore an additional wide, deep dent, likely from the old Dodge front guard which was rusty, but still a solid piece of metal compared to the body work on a newer vehicle.

'Marty!' Philips waved as they approached.

'Mate. What's up with this?' He shoved a dirty rag in the back pocket of his overalls as he joined them.

'We need to give it the once over. Might need to get the city forensic techs out to check.'

'Did Con's old lady hit someone?'

'What makes you say Selene was driving?' Jenny knelt to scan the impact on the passenger's side door.

'Con said his missus smacked into something.' He shrugged.

'But you don't know for a fact she was driving?' She kept her eyes on the door. A mix of orange, rusty looking residue and faded blue paint were imbedded in the crease of the dent.

'Nah. Con brought it in first thing this morning. Before I opened. Left the keys under the wheel arch.'

'Could it have been parked here last night?' Jenny rose, satisfied this was the vehicle that collided with her truck, but knowing they'd need Penny to confirm.

It was probably a simple process of collecting trace samples under her instruction then shipping them back to her lab in Adelaide, but at least she'd get the chance to call her friend and check on any other evidence including the hair O'Connell already mentioned.

Marty rubbed his chin. 'I guess it could have been here all night, but that's not what Con told me.'

'No worries Marty. We'll need you to keep this vehicle away from public access, even if Con comes around asking about it.' Philips slid his notepad into the top pocket of his vest.

'It's in the bloody way here mate. Can't you tow it somewhere out of my way if I can't work on it?'

'Sorry mate. We've got nowhere to impound it securely.'

Marty swore under his breath. Jenny scanned the yard. It didn't exactly look like it was busting at the seams with work. She got the distinct impression Marty didn't want to upset Con and taking the vehicle off his hands would absolve him of any responsibility.

'We'll be as quick as we can.'

'I'll call Penny and see what she needs. We can probably get it all for her and send it.'

'Good plan.'

She heard Philips start talking about footy and the up-and-coming golf game against the SES as she strolled away to stand by the vehicle mobile booster to get the best signal.

Dialling the forensic lab's number, she waited. It was Friday. Penny should be at work, unless she was on night duty.

'What you got?' Jenny was unprepared, expecting the usual phone greeting.

'Hey. You got caller ID in there now?'

'Always did have it, but I recognise your mobile now.'

'Cool.' She got straight to the point, not wanting to keep Marty waiting any longer than necessary. 'I've got a vehicle here we need to do a trace on for evidence it hit another vehicle. What do you need?'

'What vehicle and what did it hit?' There was suspicion in Penny's voice and Jenny knew she wasn't going to be able to keep the near miss from her friend like she wanted to.

'It's one of our suspect's vehicles and it nearly hit me and Nick last night outside the motel restaurant.'

'Shit Jenny. You two okay?'

'Fine. It just scared the crap out of us. But you know as well as I do when someone goes to this extent, they are likely worried I'm getting too close.'

'Yes, but why you? Why not the rest of the team?'

It was a good question and one she hadn't considered. Was this personal?

'Problem for another day. What do I need to do?'

Penny gave her a series of instructions on what to put the samples in, how to take them without contaminating them, what photos to take and how to label them properly.

'Got it. Anything new on the case we should know? O'Connell said you found a long thick hair. Anything else come up with it?'

'It was super thick. If you can find me a sample of someone's hair you think it could be, I can ID it for you. Each person's hair composition is unique. On its own, it's difficult to do more than confirm ethnicity of the host, but with a sample, I can do a match under a microscope.'

'But it was long. Curly or straight?'

'Long, straight, thick, likely a dark colour when it was left on the victim.'

'On its own, it isn't exactly conclusive though. Franny could have picked it up from anyone?'

'True, but I found it wrapped between the victim's fingers. Much like the victim grabbed a handful of hair during a fight.'

Jenny bit her lip. 'That's fairly conclusive then.'

'All I can do is give you what I know. It's up to you and your team to put the pieces together.'

'Thanks Penny. I'll catch up soon.' She went to hang up, then stopped. 'Oh, forgot to tell you. I've got some news on the hunt for Melanie.'

'Sounds promising.'

'Yeah. If it comes through, I'll let you know.'

'Deal. Gotta run.'

'Me too.' Jenny hung up, switched her phone to camera and started taking photos as she talked Philips through the process required to collect the samples needed to prove Con, Selene or maybe Tina tried to run her over.

# Chapter 44

Jenny parked outside the tiny airport terminal. Glancing at her watch, she confirmed she was running late for her lunch with Nick. Typing out a quick text, she hit *send* and stashed her phone in her front vest pocket as a regional airline plane taxied to the terminal.

A cardboard box, clearly labelled with evidence tape sat on her passenger seat. Lifting it, she jumped out the driver's side and ran for the airline counter to book her freight in before the plane loaded and lifted off.

'Officer. Got your call. We're ready for it.' A bubbly airline steward with a bright red suit and purple scarf handed her a docket to sign.

'Thanks Michelle. Efficient as usual.' Jenny passed the box over the counter and signed the paperwork. Her eyes caught something on Michelle's desk.

The air steward glanced where Jenny was looking and covered up the details. She wasn't being difficult. No doubt client paperwork was confidential, but Jenny's mind raced over what she saw on the booking form.

'Catch you later Michelle. Thanks again.'

'No worries.' The woman waved, then lifted a two-way radio handset to organise a baggage handler to load the parcel.

Jenny needed to relay what she spotted and quickly. The police radio was monitored by radio enthusiasts and journalist alike, so she used her mobile to call the station.

'Coober Pedy Police. Senior Constable O'Connell speaking.'

'Sir. I've just dropped the evidence off at the airport and saw a booking form for Selene and Tina Papadakis on Michelle's desk.'

'Roger that Williams. Philips was already on his way out to bring them in for questioning in any case. But while they are here, we'll make it perfectly clear they can't leave town until this case is done.'

'Thanks.' Jenny hung up, slipped in behind the wheel and started the Police Landcruiser. She was missing something. The makings of a headache pulsed behind her eyes as she drove out of the parking area and onto the main road.

Mentally, she ticked off what they knew.

Tina was adopted. Jason was her godfather and arranged her adoption to Con and Selene. It was quite possible, with the funds going into Franny's account that she was blackmailing three possible fathers. But they had no evidence yet. Only conjecture.

They needed to confirm who was putting money into the bank accounts. And she wanted to be at the station when they interviewed Selene and Tina. Lunch was going to have to be cancelled but she didn't want to call Nick. Instead, she drove past the motel on her way back to the station.

Running down the veranda, past the half-finished reception area and on through the restaurant doors, she spotted Nick talking with Marj as she entered. The bar was a hive of activity already, with knock off drinks for the miners starting early.

Nick waved when he saw her enter. She waved back – he must have interpreted the look on her face. 'You can't stay?'

'I can't stay. I'm *so* sorry. We have some interviews to conduct and I need to run through some video footage urgently.'

'You work too hard luv.' Marj smiled up from the seat alongside Nick.

'I'm trying to catch Franny's killer Marj.'

'They've been loose for five years. I don't think another few days will make much difference.'

'You'd be surprised.' She didn't want to blow Marj's theory apart, but most of all, she didn't want to get the rumour mill going.

Marj stood to leave, but Jenny thought of something and put her hand on her arm. 'Actually. I'm curious about something you mentioned the other day.'

'What you need luv?' She turned to Nick. 'You better order without her,' she grinned.

'I'm sorry Nick. Can we grab dinner?' Nick stood and strolled around the table.

'You still need to eat. I'll bring something over to the station for you.' He squeezed her arm.

'That would be awesome.' She grabbed his hand as he let go. 'Thanks for understanding.'

'I get it. You'd be off with the fairies if I forced you to stay anyway.' He turned and wandered between tables toward the front bar to order.

'What's going on?' Marj ushered her to take a seat.

'How well do you know Selene?'

'We aren't close, but I'm quite a few years older than her and she confides in me occasionally. This town's population is seriously skewed to men. Us girls have to stick together.' Marj's expression was infectious.

'You told me Franny was alive after Tina argued with her the night you believe she lost her earring.' Marj nodded. 'Do you know what they argued about?'

'No, sorry. I didn't hear the details, but I assume it was about the adoption. Tina spoke to me about it afterward.'

'What time was that?'

'They met before the Business Association meeting.'

'Did you see Selene at all that night?'

212

'I don't know for sure, because I didn't go, but Selene often went to the Business Association meetings with Con.' Jenny scolded herself for not having taken the time to read the minutes last night. She was shaken up over the near-miss and totally forgot.

'Thanks Marj.' Jenny slid her chair back, stood and turned all in one smooth motion, narrowly missing Nick as he approached. 'Whoops. Sorry.' Her chest was up against his, her hands out to the side like she was avoiding a brick wall.

He smiled, leant forward, and gently kissed her. 'I've ordered your lunch. I'll bring it over when it's ready.'

She wrapped her suspended arms around his neck, kissed him back, then reluctantly let go.

'Thanks.'

# Chapter 45

Jenny stepped out of the vehicle, adjusted her taser and pistol absently, as her mind tried to put pieces of the puzzle together.

Philips pulled up with Tina and Selene as Jenny opened the station door. Selene's voice was raised as she stepped from the passenger's seat of Police vehicle.

'I can't believe you people. Haven't you caused us enough stress?'

'Tina. Mrs Papadakis.' It was the first-time Jenny had heard Selene raise her voice. Up until now, she was sullen, quiet, even withdrawn, but her hands were waving in the air and her usually perfectly styled hair appeared ruffled, like she just woke up.

Maybe she had?

'And you!' Selene turned on Jenny as soon as the greeting left her lips. 'You've been digging around where you're not welcome. You are new in town. You have no right!'

A few people passing by crossed to the other side of the road to avoid Selene's rant.

'Mrs Papadakis. How about you come inside, grab a cup of tea and we can sort this all out.' Jenny gently reached for Selene's elbow. The woman dragged it free, hugging it to her chest defiantly.

Jenny frowned at Tina who apologised with her eyes, then reached out for her mum and wrapped her arms around her shoulder.

'It's okay mum. We'll be back home in time to make dinner. Let's go and help the police.' Tina spoke softly, cooing to her mother like a child.

O'Connell peered over his glasses as they entered, Selene still swearing, in a mixture of Greek and English. Jenny glanced at Gwen, then the Senior Constable and back again.

'Take them to the interview room.' O'Connell pointed to the rear of the building as Gwen asked questions, which O'Connell declined to answer. Focussed back on the Papadakis women, Jenny ushered them down the hallway to the interview room.

'I'll get you a cup of tea. Philips will stay with you.' She flashed a sympathetic look at her partner whose face told her he wished he came up with the ruse first.

As soon as she closed the door, she scooted down the hallway back to the main office. She arrived in time to see Gwen stomping out.

'Everything okay?' Jenny asked as she searched the computer for the video footage from the bank.

'She's fishing for a story. I told her we'd give a statement once we made an arrest.' O'Connell watched her typing furiously. 'What's up?'

'I've got a hunch, but I need the bank footage before I speak with Tina and Selene and it's still not here. Any chance you can make a cup of tea for them?'

O'Connell lifted his eyebrows, but turned toward the staffroom without complaint. She scanned the details, then called the local branch number. It was a long shot, but if she was right, she had a pretty good idea what was going on and who killed Franny – and more importantly, why.

The branch manager picked up. 'This is Constable Williams from the local police. We emailed a request for branch video footage, but it hasn't arrived. We urgently require the footage from the Friday before last. Can you get someone onto it immediately?'

She resisted the urge to bite her fingernails. Instead, she picked up a pen and nibbled on the end. 'I'll wait.'

O'Connell came back from the rear of the building as Sarge stepped out of his office.

'They have their tea. Now you need to explain.' O'Connell's tone caused Sergeant Mackenzie to squint in her direction.

Jenny put her finger up as the bank manager returned and started speaking. 'Yes I'm here.' She saw O'Connell join Sarge. They were a pigeon pair, with their hands on their hips and an unamused expression on their lips.

'Thanks. I wouldn't be calling if it wasn't urgent. I appreciate it.' She hung up to the sound of yelling from the back of the station.

'Sounds like the cuppa didn't do the trick.' Jenny rushed to the hallway, O'Connell and Sergeant Mackenzie right behind her.

She opened the interview door to find Selene wailing and Tina trying unsuccessfully to console her. Philips lifted his hands palms up and shrugged his shoulders helplessly.

'Tina.' The younger woman lifted her eyes at the sound of Jenny's voice. 'Is there a doctor we should call for your mum?'

She shook her head and patted her mother's shoulders. 'She'll settle down soon.'

'Does this happen often?' Sarge and O'Connell hung back in the hallway as Jenny stepped into the pokey interview room.

'No. She's not been like this for years.'

'We'll give you a minute.' Jenny waved for Philips to follow them out of the interview room. As soon as she pulled the door closed, Philips, O'Connell and Sergeant Mackenzie rounded on her.

'Start explaining Williams.' Sarge's gruff tone was back in full force.

She puffed out a quick breath. 'I'm only speculating at this stage. I need the bank footage to be sure. Then I think I can get our suspects to provide the rest of the evidence we need to convict a killer.'

The only problem was, she still wasn't positive who the killer was.

# Chapter 46

Sergeant Mackenzie's mouth opened, then closed. He rounded on Philips and O'Connell who shrugged.

'What are you expecting to find in the footage?' Sarge pursed his lips, not hiding his irritation at being left out of the loop again. Visions of the whiteboard flashed before her eyes and she realised she was operating outside guidelines again.

Taking a breath, she backtracked to bring her boss up to date. 'Three people were putting money into Franny's account, every month, on the second Friday.' Sarge nodded he knew as much. 'It hasn't stopped.'

'Someone is still putting a grand in each month?'

'Not just someone Sir,' Philips interrupted, 'I was going to tell you, then we got called out, but the thousand-dollar deposits, from three different sources, all on the same day each month, never stopped coming. We requested local branch footage because we narrowed them down to local cash deposits.'

'So whoever killed Franny, isn't one of the people she was blackmailing?' O'Connell strode down the hallway toward the main office, Sarge right behind him. Jenny and Philips followed.

'Exactly, so whoever Franny was blackmailing, likely Tina's possible fathers, can't be our killer. I want to see the footage to know who to eliminate for sure, but I think we can use it in our interview.'

'And you think Tina or Selene might have killed Franny?'

'Maybe. Marj said Tina was seen in the office the night Franny died. She lost an earring at the scene, but Marj confirms she left after some sort of fight but Franny was unharmed.'

218

'But she could have come back.' Sarge pulled the whiteboard out. O'Connell picked up the marker pen and began scribbling details down.

'Yes, or she could have gone home and spoken with her mother about the fight. We know Tina is aware of the adoption, but was she before Franny told her? How angry would Selene have been if she wasn't the one to tell her?'

'My head is spinning.' Philips leant against the door frame into the Sergeant's office.

'Philips, check to see if video from the bank has arrived yet?' He nodded, but moved slowly, reluctant to leave the debriefing. O'Connell pulled the top from his marker pen and added Selene's name to the whiteboard.

'Plus, Marj told me earlier Selene was likely at the Business Association meeting the night Franny died. I just need to finish checking over the minutes.'

'And it sounds like she might be the one who tried to run you over.' Sarge snorted air through his nostrils. 'But I can't believe she would kill Franny.'

'Sir, it's been bugging me all this time why anyone would dispose of the victim in the office wall and not just drag the body outside and load it in a van and dump it in a mine somewhere.'

'And?'

'They might have been interrupted, but then the body would have been found, so I'm guessing, the killer was small, too small or weak to drag Franny's body out.'

'That makes sense.'

'They also needed to have experience with plastering or some sort of trade.'

'I'm not going to ask again. Get on with it Williams.'

Jenny grinned. 'Selene renovated the dugout they live in, virtually on her own from all accounts. There are photos in the house of her covered in plaster and paint.'

'You, with me Williams.' Sarge wiggled his finger. 'We need to interview Tina and Selene apart.'

'Sir, I've checked through the Friday morning footage.' Philips met the Sergeant at his office door.

'What have you found?'

'Con, Dragan and Alexi, all at the bank the same day as the deposits.'

'It could be a coincidence.'

'It could be, but I rang the bank manager back and asked him to see if they could get times on the deposits. They can, it will take some time, but we should be able to prove it.'

'Selene won't know we don't have proof.' Jenny smirked at Sarge until a wicked grin crossed his face.

'I like the way you think Williams.'

'Sir. I need to check the minutes before we do the interview.' Jenny picked up a pile of paperwork from a tray at the front counter. 'There's also one more thing before we go in.' She scanned the minutes, her eyes focussed as she kept speaking. 'I spoke with Penny earlier today.'

Sarge waited near the hallway to the interview room and cells.

'O'Connell told us about the hair Penny found.' He nodded, 'Sir, it was wrapped in her hand and buried inside the wall with her. Like she yanked it out of someone's head when she died.'

'And you think it might be the killer's?'

'This is interesting.' Jenny frowned, looked up, then returned her gaze to the paperwork. 'Selene was an apology for the Business Association meeting on the night of Franny's murder.'

'It's not looking good for her.'

'We can't walk in and expect to get a hair sample, but I've got an idea.'

Voices in the foyer drew everyone's attention. Jenny's heart sank as she recognised the deep baritone voice.

'I'd like to see my clients *now*.'

'Alexi. I thought you retired from legal practice when you became Mayor?' Sarge strolled to the counter, his posture relaxed, his tone calm.

'It seems the police have a vendetta against the Papadakis family and since Tina is my future wife, I thought it best to offer my services.' His smarmy expression made Jenny's blood curdle.

'Tina and Selene are only helping with our enquires, but here, let me show you through.' He lifted the countertop and bowed slightly, his hand ushering the Mayor in. As Alexi turned his back to Jenny, Sarge rolled his eyes, his lips were tightly pursed. He wasn't happy. She wasn't sure if he was annoyed with Alexi, or her.

# Chapter 47

Jenny caught up to Alexi before they reached the interview room, a thought popping into her head. She reached out, resting her hand on the doorknob.

'Actually, before we go in, are you sure you want to represent Tina and Selene?' Sarge's frown matched Alexi's.

'Of course. Why wouldn't I?'

'Because you could be Tina's biological father and that is just ewww.' Jenny screwed up her nose. 'But by all means, let's do this.' She lifted her hand to open the door.

Alexi's hand sprang on top of hers. 'What do you mean?'

'We have video of you putting money into Franny's account, every month for the past decade, maybe more. I'm assuming it's because she possessed damning information and I'm only guessing, but a DNA test can easily confirm – you're Tina's father.'

'You wouldn't dare?'

'So you aren't denying an affair with Franny?' Alexi's lip lifted in a snarl. Sarge stepped forward, reminding the Mayor he was right there, ready to defend Jenny.

'Marrying your daughter is a crime in this country Alexi. We are obliged to tell Tina so she can undergo a DNA test. You can be in the room if you like?'

'Or not!' Jenny added as she turned the knob to open the door.

Sarge followed her into the interview room, Alexi did not. 'Mrs Papadakis, we have some new evidence in the Franny Kovac case and we'll need to interview you and Tina separately.'

'If you can come with me Mrs Papadakis.' Sarge stepped up next to the older woman, gripped her arm gently and coaxed her from her seat. 'I'm going to read you your rights, give you time to speak with your lawyer, but we are holding you under the suspicion of murder.'

'No. You can't.' Tina rushed to her feet. 'Mum isn't stable enough to be interviewed.'

When Con mentioned Selene was sick, from all the stress, Jenny wondered if there might be an underlying medical condition, but the way the woman acted when Philips brought her in, only fuelled the idea.

Now, Tina was basically spelling it out for them.

'Is your mother on medication?' Jenny whispered.

Tina shook her head and watched as Sergeant Mackenzie handed her over to Philips in the hallway. 'Take Mrs Papadakis to my office and allow Alexi to speak with his client. We'll only be a minute. We have a few questions for Tina first.'

Tina swallowed hard, holding back tears as Jenny sat and waited for Sarge to close the door and start the recording.

'I'm sorry Tina. How long has she been ill?'

'I don't know to be honest. She has good days, months, even years, then something stressful happens and she melts down.'

'Tina, what did you and Franny argue about the night she died?'

The question must have been unexpected. Tina's eyes widened. She licked her lips, delaying the answer.

'I met Franny a few times, socially. She was always nice to me, but that night...' Tina's hands fidgeted in her lap, 'that night she told me I was her daughter, adopted out at birth.'

'Did you already know you were adopted?'

'No. I always wondered, with my height, my build and the colour of my eyes, but,' she shrugged, 'I always figured I was a throwback genetically or something.'

'Did Franny say anything else? Marj said you argued, and you left in tears.'

'She,' Tina's eyes glistened, 'she said Alexi could be my father.'

'That must have made you angry.'

'No, just more determined not to marry him.'

'Was your mum home when you got back from the argument?' A nod. 'Did you tell her what Franny told you?' Another nod. 'Can you answer for the recording?'

'Yes, she was home. Yes I told her.'

'Everything? *All* the possible fathers?'

Tina's quick intake of breath said she did, but she didn't answer. Jenny carried on.

'Was she angry Tina?'

'Yes, she was angry. But she went to the committee meeting with dad. She can't have killed anyone. She wouldn't.' Her voice hit a high note. Her eyes scanned Jenny's face.

'She didn't go to the meeting Tina. She was an apology. I read the minutes.'

'I shouldn't have told her.'

'You couldn't have known.'

'She's been so moody, so angry since the body was found. But she couldn't have killed anyone.'

'I think we are done here.' Sarge stopped the recording. 'Let's get you signed out Tina and we'll start interviewing your mum, if Alexi is ready.' His chair slid back. Tina remained seated.

Jenny rose and rounded the interview desk, 'Come on Tina. We'll need a DNA test from you if we can, to confirm paternity.' She gently eased Tina from the chair. 'The good news is, if Alexi is your father, the wedding will definitely be off.' Jenny smiled. It wasn't returned.

Sarge opened the door. Jenny wrapped her arm around Tina, steering her out. 'Why were you going along with the wedding if you knew Alexi could be your father?'

As they reached the end of the hallway, tingles ran down Jenny's spine. A mixture of voices… heated, confused, and loud filtered her way. She released her arm from Tina, realising she still wore her duty weapon.

So did Philips. They were so focussed on the case, neither of them put their gun away in the safe.

'I'll kill him. I will.' Jenny caught Sarge's gaze. She tapped her weapon and nudged Tina toward him before peering around the corner to see what was going on.

Selene shielded herself behind Alexi, a pistol aimed at his gut. Her eyes were wildly searching the room. 'Where is that stuck up little bitch?'

'Mrs Papadakis. Put the gun down.' Philips held his hands up. His holster was empty, but his taser was still mounted to his utility vest.

Jenny remembered her taser. Flicking the safety off, she left it on her vest, then grasped her gun with two hands.

'Selene. Please!' Alexi begged.

'Don't you dare. You, Con, Dragan. How many more men did that slut sleep with?'

Jenny peeked around the corner once more. Alexi was right in front of Selene, his eyes wide, sweat beading on his brow. His eyes scanned the room, begging anyone to help him.

The site was almost comical. Small, petite Selene, holding a bulky man like Alexi at gun point. But there was nothing humorous about the situation. Selene was capable of murder. Of that she was now sure.

'Where is she?' Selene's voice was bordering on hysterics.

'Are you looking for me Mrs Papadakis?' Jenny stepped out from the hallway, away from cover. She heard Sarge protest from behind her, but ignored him. Selene wanted her. Why, she didn't know but she wanted to find out.

'Why are you so angry with me Selene?' Jenny held her hands out at her side, the gun still in her hand.

Selene saw it, licked her lips then her eyes fixed on Jenny's. 'You. You come in, all pretty and free to do whatever you want and start snooping around.'

'I'm a police officer Selene. It's what I do.'

'You're just like her.'

'Franny?' Jenny failed to see how the independent journalist who slept with half the town was anything like her, but she needed to engage the woman, so Philips could get to his taser.

Jenny's weapon was no use. Alexi was too big a shield in front of the woman.

'Drop your gun!' Selene screamed.

'How about I holster it?'

'Drop it, push it over there.' Selene nodded to the far side of the room.

'What's the plan Selene? We've alerted the airport. I saw your tickets already. You can't fly.'

Selene frowned with confusion. Did she book the flights? Maybe Tina did? Jenny peered over her shoulder. Did she have it all wrong? One look at Tina made her sure she didn't. Her eyes were brimming with tears. Her whole body shook. Sarge held her firmly with his arm wrapped tightly around her shoulder.

'The gun. Push it away.'

Jenny made eye contact with Philips. As Selene's focus tracked her weapon, slowly being lowered to the floor, Philips' focus was on her other hand, tapping her taser.

He nodded. His hands still held high in the air. Jenny kicked the gun away from Philips, toward O'Connell's desk. It slid along the floor. Selene's eyes followed it as she hoped. Philips seized the opportunity, reaching down, he flicked the switch on his taser, throwing his hand back up before Selene saw.

Jenny held her breath. O'Connell sat at his desk, behind the computer. His eyes tracked the weapon as it slid his way, stopping out of easy reach.

'What do you want Selene? You killed Franny. You can't expect to get away with that?'

'I want my daughter. Where's Tina?'

'She's safe.'

'Tina!'

'She's scared Mrs Papadakis. You are scaring her.' Jenny studied Philips, Alexi, the gun. It was all too close, too risky right now. They needed the gun pointing somewhere else, not at Alexi's torso.

'Tina. I love you baby. Come on out. We need to go. I did this all for you. For us.' Selene's expression was tormented.

Jenny glanced back at Tina around the corner in the hallway, out of her mother's sight. 'What else did Franny tell you Tina?'

'I need to calm her down. She'll stop for me.' Tina tried to move forward, but Sarge held her back.

'I want my daughter!' Selene screamed. Alexi squirmed. She jabbed the gun into his ribs. He grunted.

'Mum. I'm okay. I'm here.' She tugged, trying to free her arm from Sarge's grip. Her eyes pleading.

Jenny shrugged at her boss. This was his call. Sarge studied Tina, then glanced at her, finally, he reluctantly let his hand slip away. 'Just be careful,' he whispered.

Jenny put her hand up, stopping Tina from moving into view of her mother. 'Tell me what Franny said Tina.'

'She said she would take me away from all this crap. She didn't give me up for an arranged marriage.'

Jenny let her hand drop. Tina stepped into view. 'I thought you were against Tina marrying Alexi?' Jenny studied Selene's face, waiting for an answer.

'I was.'

'But you didn't want her to move away either?'

Tears formed in Selene's eyes, her gun-hand relaxed. 'Mum. It's okay.' She stepped forward. 'Let Alexi go. I won't marry him. I won't leave town either. I promise.'

Everyone in the room held their breath. Alexi's eyes scanned faces, desperate to find someone with a solution to his problem.

Tina crept forward another step. Selene's eyes softened as she let the gun face the floor. Philips remained rigid, his hands still in the air, but they were lower, ready to move. Jenny fought the urge to move in, gently shaking her head to tell Philips it wasn't safe yet. Selene still held the gun.

'Hey!' Nick's voice made Jenny's blood run cold. He was bringing her lunch. 'Sorry it took...'

'Get back Nick!' she screamed. He dropped the paper bag. Selene's eyes went wild. The gun lifted in Nick's direction.

Jenny's heart raced, time slowed, she was running before any conscious thought descended on her brain.

The gun fired, she jumped, the thud to her chest felt like a sledgehammer.

'Jenny!' Nick's voice echoed.

The sound of screaming and a crackle filled her ears as she fought the pain in her chest. Nick's voice sounded soft against the pulsing of blood in her ears. 'Are you okay?'

'Vest,' she smiled as she gazed punch drunk around the front office.

Selene convulsed on the floor, taser wires hung in the air. Alexi was on his knees, on the floor, sobbing. Tina was crying, wrapped in Sarge's powerful grip as she clawed to reach her mother. O'Connell was on his feet, cuffs in hand, reaching for Selene as the taser pulsing stopped. Philips was white as a ghost. His eyes fixed on the woman at his feet.

Jenny felt hands on her body, running all over her trying to find any blood. 'You're alright.' Nick dragged her into his arms breathlessly, kissing her eyes, her cheeks, her lips.

When he stopped, she spoke softly, trying to find the energy to move. 'I told you, the vest.' She limply tapped her chest.

'Now I know how you felt when I was shot.' The vision of blood pooling around Nick's body made her shudder. He had no idea, but she said nothing. Smiling weakly, she mustered the strength to return his embrace.

# Chapter 48

Jenny sat back in her seat, enjoying the hum of noise and voices along with the smell of beer and fried food. Nick's lips tilted in a shy grin. His rare smile always made her tummy tingle.

'A toast, to Jenny not dying today.' Nev lifted his beer. Tim and he raced to see who would finish first.

'I'll drink to that.' Sarge and O'Connell tapped schooner glasses.

Jenny's eyes rested on Philips next to her. 'You okay?'

A faint smile touched his lips. 'I'm good.'

'I was worried about you. You looked so white. Was it using the taser?' She leant over so only he could hear.

He shrugged. 'Let's say I'm glad it wasn't my pistol, but no, seeing you dive in front of a bullet is what drained the blood from my body.'

'I had my vest on.'

'Jenny, a hundred mil higher and it would have hit your neck.'

She touched her throat. He was right, but at the time, in that moment, she didn't even recall she was wearing a vest. It was a gun, pointed at someone she cared about. It was a bullet she'd take again any day, with or without the vest.

'So what happened after I left?' Jenny scanned O'Connell and Sarge's faces. 'Tim wouldn't let me leave the ambulance until I was fully checked. I missed all the fun.' She grinned at her roommate who raised his glass in salute.

'We formally charged Selene. Sent a sample of her hair away for matching by the lab, but we pretty much have her confession. Either way, she's going to jail for drawing a

230

weapon on a police officer.' Sarge refilled his glass from the beer jug.

'And Tina, did she know her mum killed Franny? I think she booked the airfares, not her mum?' Jenny sipped her beer and wiped the frothy head from her lip.

'She might have had a suspicion, but we've not pressed charges. She was only eighteen. Franny offered to take her away from all the arranged marriage thing but she didn't want to leave her mum or Tom.'

'They've been together that long? Why go ahead with the marriage then?'

'Tradition? Family honour? Who knows.' O'Connell shrugged. 'Honestly beats me. Marriage is overrated anyway.'

Jenny thought of Gwen, a question on her lips was lost as a voice spoke behind her.

'How's it all going?' The sound was familiar, she glanced over her shoulder, as Nev spoke.

'Hey Sis. What you doing here?' Nev slid his chair back and shimmied around the table between chairs to hug her. He often kept his accent hidden, but seeing Nellie must have made him fall back to it. As an Indigenous doctor, he walked between two worlds – that of the original custodians and the European settlers who now ruled it.

'Meet one of my mob. This is Nellie.' He introduced her to everyone. She smiled, white teeth shining brightly.

'Hi everyone.' Her eyes fell on Jenny. 'Can I interrupt a sec?'

'Sure. What's up?' Jenny half stood, her stomach filling with butterflies. *She's heard back from Melanie.*

'It's okay.' Nellie put her hand on Jenny's shoulder. 'Stay here. I've got something for you.' She rushed toward the front of the motel restaurant.

Hot tears stung Jenny's eyes. Her nose ran instantly as goose bumps covered her skin. Standing by the entrance, with a young boy at her side was Melanie. There was no mistaking the petite, pretty face staring back at her. For the first time ever, Jenny noticed how unsure and nervous that face appeared.

'Oh my god.' She flung the chair back so fast, Nick had to reach for it to stop it hitting the floor. Her eyes darted to him, back to Melanie and back at him again.

'It's her. It's Mel!' Voices spoke around her. She vaguely heard Sarge say something. Then Philips. Nick's hand found hers and squeezed. 'It's really her.' She stumbled as she tried to close the distance to her cousin. Nick wrapped his arm round her, propping her up as she staggered forward.

Melanie was fixed to the spot. The boy's uncertain eyes watched Mel, then Jenny, then Mel again.

'Jen!' Melanie finally moved, dragging the boy toward her. 'I'm so sorry.' She reached for Jenny, Jenny grabbed her, hugging her so tightly Melanie's words were muffled against her chest. The bruises from the bullet earlier stung, but she ignored them.

'You're alive. I was afraid I'd never see you again. Where have you been?' There were so many questions running through her mind.

'It's a long story. I'm so sorry. I should have...'

'It's okay. Really it's okay.' Jenny noticed brown eyes staring up at her. 'Who's this?'

'Tristan, meet your Aunt Jenny.' The idea of being an aunt made Jenny lightheaded. Nick squeezed her arm, bringing her back to reality.

'This is Nick. He owns the William Creek Station.'

Nick leant forward and whispered. 'I would have opened with *this is my boyfriend*, but you get the idea.' Mel grinned.

Jenny was too stunned to speak for a moment, but found her words when her eyes met Mel's once more.

'Where have you been?' she said again.

'Mum's coming in tomorrow. We'll talk then.'

'Come and meet my friends.' Jenny led Melanie and her son to the table. Chairs shuffled to make room for two more. Jenny's heart was beating so fast she thought it might explode. Melanie was alive. Aunt Carolyn was alive. But the niggling questions remained.

*Why did they run away nearly ten years ago?*

*And why not tell her where they were going?*

********

Thanks for reading! I hope you enjoyed *Her Hidden Bones*. I'd love to see your review on your favourite online bookstore.

*Her Lonely Bones* - Book 5 in the *Opal Field* series will be available soon from all good bookstores. If you would like to learn more about my writing or what's next in Jenny's story, then visit my website www.atime2write.com.au.

You'll also find me on Facebook and Instagram along with Goodreads and other online book fan website. Join me for the rest of Jenny's adventure.